McCALL

McCall

•

Robert H. Redding

AVALON BOOKS
NEW YORK

PRINTED IN THE UNITED STATES OF AMERICA
ON ACID-FREE PAPER
BY HADDON CRAFTSMEN, BLOOMSBURG, PENNSYLVANIA

McCALL

Chapter One

McCall cocked his .45 Colt long-barrel. He pointed it at two men in dirty chaps and scuffed boots.

"You," he said, "are dead."

"You wouldn't shoot us?" gasped one.

"We ain't armed," pleaded the other, his pale eyes wide with fright.

"You were," McCall reminded him, nodding at a couple of pistols lying on the sandy ground. He laughed, a dry, bitter sound. "No," he went on, "I want to see you both do a dance—at the end of a hangman's rope, legally. Now get on your horses. We're heading for town."

The trio mounted, McCall trailing closely.

"We got the last of them around here, Dogs," he informed his horse, a black gelding, with fierce, opaque eyes. "The rest got away." He puckered his lips and spat. "We still got work to do."

"Our brother, Turk, will get you for this," yelled one of the men.

"You mean that robbing killer down south?" McCall spat again. The sun was hot, and his brow was beaded with sweat. "Oh, I'm worried," he grunted. "Really worried."

"He'll get you if we hang," came the promise.

"And I'll get you, if you don't. Think about it, you punks."

It was ten miles to town. A tip from the Rainbow's bartender put him onto these men, among the last bad ones in the statewide Rustler's War.

"They are Dug and Handy Siderack," the bartender had told him. "They come in here to wet their tonsils. I heard 'em say they was dug in at Castle Rock."

And it was at the Rock that McCall surprised them.

He leaned on the pommel of his saddle. "You know who killed my wife and child?"

The question was released with suppressed anger, but an anger so great that his two captives shuddered.

"You ast us that already," muttered the one called Dug.

"And I'll ask again," came the slow, terrible voice. "And again—until I find out."

The two mumbled jerkily to each other. Then the one called Handy offered, "We don't know nothin' firsthand, but what's it to you if we give you a couple of names?"

McCall rode forward, drawing his heavy pistol. He lashed out savagely, and Handy crumpled in the saddle.

"Hey," shouted Dug, "what'd you do that fer? We was just offerin' help."

"He asked what it was worth if he gave names—so I showed him." McCall fired his weapon, and Dug's hat toppled from his head. "If the names don't strike me as any good"—he lowered the barrel of his weapon a few inches—"that's what they're worth."

The stunned Handy stirred and sat upright. He was bleeding from a cut, and bleary-eyed. "All's I wanted to know," he sputtered, "is would you speak a good word to the judge if we told what we thought?"

McCall stifled a murderous impulse to shoot them right then. For all he knew, the two before him had killed his family. He trusted no outlaw's word, but he controlled himself. "I promise no deals," he told the man. "I'm only a posse member."

"Ah," countered Dug, "we know you. You practically led them lawmen by yourself. They look up to you. You can help us."

"Speak up," growled McCall, "or I'll kill you both, and laugh while you bleed."

"Well, they was Blake and Scar, mebbe," muttered Handy.

"Them two, well, they liked killin', and I heard 'em say somethin'."

The captive rustler hesitated.

McCall grabbed the man's arm with a large hand and squeezed. "Speak," he ordered, "or I'll break that scrawny thing in two."

Handy squeaked in pain, then hurried on. "I heard 'em say, they was going t' clean out the next place. No witnesses left."

"And?" The hand tightened.

"And your place was next, because you was causin' so much trouble."

McCall thought back. He was on business that day in Postville, the area's center. It was when he returned that he found his wife and daughter dead, his ranch house pillaged and burned.

"But we wasn't in on that," whined Handy. "We was at the other end of the world."

"Meaning you were stealing cattle at some other ranch."

The two fell into a sullen silence, except for one grumbled statement from Handy. "Remember, you promised to help us."

"I promised nothing," was the stony reply.

Handy and his brother, Dug, were hanged three days later. The judge, a man who also served as postmaster and coroner, knew the two. As did most people in the region, he knew many of the gang who had precipitated the Rustler's War.

"You two," he addressed the pair, "were a part of the most heinous bunch of rats ever to disgrace the name of rats. I don't know why McCall didn't shoot you on sight—shows he had more compassion than most of us, and with far less reason."

"We give him names," protested Handy.

"Might help him get them as kilt his fambly."

" 'Might' is a big word here," returned the judge. "You are criminals. Why should we take your word for anything! No, gentlemen, your record of rustling, robbery and murder,"—the judge fairly shook with anger as he spoke—"don't allow for any mercy. You will hang."

McCall watched the pair as they did their dance of death at the end of stout hemp ropes. He felt some satisfaction, but the awful grief that filled his being allowed no peace.

He returned to his ranch and looked it over sadly. There were two graves in the shade of a great tree. They were marked simply, "Belle McCall, a loving wife," and "Katherine McCall, a brave, darling daughter." It was all the legend he felt necessary. He stood by the graves, flat Stetson in hand, and wept in his heart for the loss of the only family he had, the most important people in his life.

"I will get them," he said quietly, "and that is the promise of my life."

He went to a shed where he had set up living quarters. He packed a few things into his saddlebags, mounted Dogs, and left for Postville.

In town he went to the bank.

"I want to sell the Bar M," he told the banker. "Know of any buyers?"

The banker, a man dressed entirely in black and with an undertaker's attitude toward life, came out of character with a shouted, "Sell! Man, you can't. We need you around here."

"I'm selling," McCall insisted quietly, "except for one piece of the ground."

"Which is?"

"The place where my wife and daughter are buried. That will remain mine."

The banker shook his head. "McCall, it was you who cleaned them rustlers out."

"I had a lot of help."

"Yes—but you led the way. You outfoxed them devils. It was you who did it. This here region needs you." The banker grew confidential. "I heard there's talk of running you for governor. We need a leader like you."

"Governors are appointed by politicians in Washington," McCall reminded the banker.

"Yeah," the man grinned, "but who do you think backs the politicians?"

McCall nodded. He knew how things were done.

"Thanks," he said dryly, "but I've more important work to do." His voice hardened. "I'm selling. I want no more of this place." He was bitter again. "I could never live here after what happened. Every day of my life I'd be reminded of my wife and daughter." He rapped gently but ever so firmly on the banker's desk. "Either you know of a buyer, or I'll look elsewhere."

The banker sighed. He pressed the tips of his fingers together and looked squarely into McCall's burning eyes. "To tell the truth," he said, "I'd do the same as you. All right, I'll find a buyer. In spite of the Rustler's War, people still want to move in."

In another three days, McCall sold his ranch to a couple newly arrived from the East. He demanded his provision be written into the contract, that the ground in which his wife and daughter lay buried remain his.

"And I'll watch over the graves," promised the woman, who knew the story. "I'll keep them nice."

McCall thanked her for that, and with money from the sale in his pocket, he mounted Dogs and left. He had no idea where to go.

"But I heard there's a lot of new ranches opening in the north Plains country," he reflected. "That's where rustlers would gather." His eyes fired up. "Killers, I mean. Yeah, Dogs, we'll head north."

And Dogs, perfect horse that he was, snorted agreement and tossed his head. It didn't matter where they went, because he'd carry the man on his back anywhere. That was the way it was with the black gelding.

Chapter Two

Two weeks after the hanging of Dug and Handy, a man appeared in Postville, a powerfully built man, not overly tall, but barrel-chested, bull-necked, with Sandow biceps. He was dark but ruddy-faced. His eyes were dark and shone with a peculiar light—the light, perhaps, that shines in the eyes of zealots and crazy people.

He was striking in general appearance, but the two things any observer noted immediately were his bearing—a thrusting forward, like a club ready to strike—and his mustache. His mustache was dark and long, and it spiraled to fine points at both ends, straight out from thick lips. From this he had gained the nickname "Turk," after prints depicting warriors of that far country, Turkey. His surname was Siderack.

He went to the Rainbow Saloon and asked the bartender who had brought in Dug and Handy.

"They are—were—my brothers," said Turk, "and I want to know."

The bartender, a friend of McCall, pretended not to know.

A man having a drink at the end of the bar said, "Come with me."

He and Turk left together. They went to a boarding house at the end of town, where they saw a man named Pete. Pete was in bed, suffering from lead poisoning. He had been shot in one of the last battles of the Rustler's War, and was hiding out in the hope of recovering.

"It was McCall," Pete told the man with the peculiar mustache.

"You sure? I want no mistakes."

"Sure? I'm sure. I know the man who shot me—an' everythin' he done since then."

"Where'd he go?"

Pete shrugged. "All's I know is he sold out and went after them as he thinks kilt his woman and child."

"His family was killed?"

"Yep."

"By who?"

"Well, I think it was Blake and Scar—I don't know their last names."

"I know them." Turk grinned, revealing straight, yellowed teeth. "Good men."

"Yeah, I guess. You goin' after McCall?"

"What's he look like?"

Pete gave a description as nearly as he could recall, right down to the pistol that had wounded him, perhaps fatally.

"That all?" Turk was doubtful. "There are a hundred men like him."

"Except for one thing," Pete added, with a sudden insight.

"What?"

"McCall will be lookin' fer the men as kilt his family, and he'll be different than the hunnert you talk about."

Turk nodded, then left without another word. He visited the graves of his brothers.

"You and me," he said to the mounds, "never was that close, but we did help when we needed each other, so I owe you this. I'll get him, and then the books are closed."

He stood quietly, for all the world like a

man in mourning, then he spat on the graves. "Punks," he muttered. "I was doing good down south."

He confirmed Pete's description of McCall from those in town willing to talk—and not many were. McCall was a hero and the town was grateful, and people were aware of Sidetrack's mission.

After another day, Turk left Postville. He had a general idea of the direction taken by his quarry—north. The trail was cold, and there would have to be much luck to ever close in on the man who had caused his brothers' deaths. It might be best to keep an ear open for the doings of Blake and Scar. Where they were, his man would be, too.

Blake and Scar were at that moment robbing a stage near Indian Territory.

They rode out into the dusty set of tracks that passed for a road with pistols drawn. To emphasize their point, they shot the driver, and his guard was forced to grab the reins.

"For pity's sake," yelled the guard. "What'd you do that fer? He'd 'av stopped."

"Shut your yap or you'll get it next," warned Scar, so called because of a jagged line across his left cheek. He peered into the coach. "All you passengers git out."

There were two women and three men aboard. They disembarked slowly, frightened and pale. None of the men, all drummers, carried weapons.

"Easy pickin's." Blake, a skinny, tall man with blond hair and close-set eyes grinned.

The two took all the cash and jewelry, and sized up the women with evil eyes.

"Look pretty good," hissed Blake.

"Yeah, what you say?"

It was then one of the men spoke. "You leave them women alone. They done you no harm."

Blake shot him in the chest. The man squawked and staggered back. Clutching at his blood-soaked shirt, he fell.

"Anybody else got somethin' to say?" Blake invited.

Before anybody could recover from the shock of what had just happened, the sound of hoofbeats drummed in the air.

"Let's git," hollered Scar, and the two leaped on their horses and fled.

Moments later, a troop of Seventh Cavalry galloped into sight.

"We've been robbed," screamed one of the women, "and two men killed."

"It was barbaric," a male passenger babbled hysterically. "Awful. They gunned down those two in cold blood."

"One have a scar?" inquired the officer in charge, a young lieutenant.

"That's him, and the other's a skinny, tall feller."

The officer nodded, and directed a trooper to see to the men who had been shot.

"We been looking for those two," said the officer. "Which way did they head?"

"Over there!"

The hysterical passenger pointed in a direction exactly opposite to the one that the murderers had taken.

The other passengers, horrified by what had taken place, a stunning event violently injected into ordinary lives, said nothing. None knew for sure which direction Blake and Scar went.

"No time to lose," barked the officer. "We want those two. Come on, men."

The troopers urged their ponies into a gallop, bent on a futile attempt, though they didn't know it.

Blake and Scar made good their escape, a fact that puzzled them slightly.

"I got a hunch they was troopers lookin'

fer Injuns off their reservations," offered Scar.

"An' us," was the sly observation.

"Yeah. We been makin' a lot of noise in these parts."

"Mebbe we ought to clear out?"

"Let's head east to the Dakotas."

"Good idea. I hear lots of people are comin' in there to mine and homestead."

"Good pickin's. Nothin' like a greenhorn from the East with their fat wallets."

"We can git us a few more boys."

"Bigger gang, the more loot."

"I hear Wolf is up here, and Butch Kelly, mebbe in Leadville."

The two rode with jaunty confidence. They had enough money to keep them in groceries for a while, so they could take their time and plan bigger jobs.

"We'll get us a bunch together," said Scar, "and in a year we'll be rich."

"Agreed," said Blake, then laughed.

"What you laughin' at?" demanded Scar, not wanting to be left out.

"And all the killin' we can do, brother." Drake's narrow eyes were glistening. "Sort of like dessert, eh?"

"Yeah," agreed the other, and his scar turned crimson with the excitement he was feeling. "Yeah."

Chapter Three

McCall traveled a zigzag trail northward. He and Dogs didn't try to burn brush, as the saying goes, but took it easy.

"I don't know why we should run fast for what might be a dry well, friend," he told his obliging horse. "We'll just poke along."

The man from the Bar M in South Texas had only a vague idea about the two men he was seeking. Blake had a hot temper, a killer's temperament. He was skinny, too. Scar carried a vivid reminder down the ragged map that nature called a face. Those were the only clues. There were a dozens of men like them.

17

He learned that the hard way.

After testing the beans and bedbugs in half a dozen towns with names like Horse's Cliff, Blue Junction, and Spider's Heaven, McCall arrived at Knife. Knife was like the rest, with a dusty street, narrow boardwalks, and false-fronted buildings. Mining had caused it to spring to life, and now mining was dying, and so was the town. Men hung around under the saloon porches, keeping as cool as possible in the shade. They watched silently as McCall rode into their privacy aboard a jaunty broomtail, black as restaurant coffee.

McCall lit in front of a saloon called the Traveler's Friend, hitched Dogs to the rail, and went in. He was thirsty. His clothes were white with alkali dust, and his hair was gritty with the same. He needed a drink, a meal, and a bath.

The man in the white apron poured him a shot, and McCall downed it. He didn't drink much, never saw the reason for it, but he did have one or two now and then, and this was an occasion for two. He was discouraged and needed some sort of a lift, even if temporary. The trail had been long, and was growing.

"Another," he ordered.

The bartender repeated the ritual.

"Well," came a sarcastic voice from the end of the bar. "Looks like our pilgrim has got himself a thirst."

"Hey," came a muted warning, "don't start with him, Prague."

"Ah, this here cow pasture needs entertainment, and I aim to git me some."

The man who uttered those uplifting words was tall and heavy. He had a scar on his face, that looked like a jagged bolt of lightning.

The moment McCall saw him, he stiffened into anger. It wasn't the ordinary anger that comes from being pestered by a nuisance. It was a deep anger, an anger that boiled up from the very wellsprings of his being. The scar! That purple, ugly scar.

Scar!

He flew into the man with a bellow that shook the two-by-six rafters. The other went for his pistol in a futile effort, an effort that died when a giant fist broke his nose. The man crumpled like a hundred-pound sack of wheat short fifty pounds. He went down and breathed heavily, looking very peaceful save for the blood trickling from his broken nose.

There were ominous clicks from several

directions, and McCall tensed, waiting for the bullets that would end his quest.

None came, but a reedy voice, full of .45 caliber authority, did.

"Now, stranger, what did yuh do that fer?"

"Because I wanted to."

"He meant no harm."

"He wanted a fight and he got one."

McCall faced the speaker carefully. "I think he killed my family."

There was a heavy silence in the room. Breathing was subdued but liquid, like an ocean tide drifting from a sandy shore.

"Where you from, stranger?"

The speaker was a short man with a narrow, dangerous face, but his eyes held a certain wisdom.

"Postville."

"Where the Rustler's War took place?"

"That's it."

"Feller, Prague ain't been farther than fifty mile from here in five years. I vouch fer that."

"All's I know is one of the killers had a scar on his face, like this gent."

"Oh, yeah." The voice was soft and reflective, "I know about him. Saw him and his friend, I think."

McCall's lost interest in the fallen fun-seeker who was bubbling through his nose.

"Where, when?"

" 'Bout three months ago. Headin' east from here. Least that's how I seen 'em go."

"His partner a skinny guy?"

"Yeah, that's him, near as I can recall."

"What's east of here?"

"Gold in the Dakotas, what I hear."

The speaker had verified, though a bit loosely, what little McCall knew about Blake and Scar. The man on the floor wasn't the one he wanted, as emphasized by the cocked pistols. He trusted the speaker with the dangerous face. That man would have shot him without a second thought if he figured Prague was in real danger. The two he sought were heading toward the big sky, where the sun came up.

McCall finished his drink, and laid five dollars on the counter.

"Drinks for everybody," he told the bartender, then turned to the spokesman, who still held his pistol. "I got no interest here. Can I go?"

The man nodded solemnly. "I reckon anybody who's on a mission like yours is going to make plenty of mistakes." He grinned at the fallen Prague. "I guess he's had plenty excitement for now."

McCall left without more words. He put Dogs in a stable and took a hotel room. He had his hot bath, and also a big meal of steak and potatoes and dried apple pie. He slept that night on a feather tick, instead of rocks and sand, but was up early.

"We got a lot of ground to cover, Dogs," he apologized, "so we got to head out early. We got to get those people, Dogs!" He thumped the horn of his saddle with such violence that Dogs glanced back, puzzled. What was that? A new order?

But the man on his back settled into his usual calm, and pointed them east.

There was more trouble after that with scar-faced men. There was something in McCall that flung him straight into trouble with them. After a while, he realized what it was: memories. The memory of his beloved wife and child returned full on, like a raging prairie fire, whenever he saw a man with a scar on his face. He couldn't seem to help himself. He was a man who prided himself on his self-control, but when it came to scar-faced men, he broke loose. He was always the winner in the fight, because his fury would not let him lose, but finding he was, once again, wrong, he was also ashamed. There were all too many faces in the upper Plains country that would probably bear the marks of his fists forever, and McCall was not proud of it. But proud or not, he tackled each suspect with a fury that could not be curbed. It would never be, until he reached the one he was after.

Stories drifted to him, like smelly breezes, about a new gang that had been formed. The new gang, so it was said, fell under the leadership of a tall, skinny fellow, who killed at the drop of a hat or less, and a man with a scar. McCall heard about the gang, but the information was sketchy. It seemed that Blake and Scar were the leaders, judging from descriptions, and their predations were terrible. There were never any witnesses left. Everybody who was robbed was killed, and so the descriptions of Blake and Scar were guesswork on the part of the public. Still, even guesswork had to have some basis in reality, and McCall traveled on hope.

He traveled easily but steadily, and finally reached the North Platte. On crossing a cattle range, he saw a ranch, and, weary, decided to pause for a meal and a bunk.

He tied up in front of a big log house, and knocked.

A young woman answered. She was dressed in a riding skirt, white blouse, and neckerchief. She was pretty, with long, auburn hair, brown eyes, and a smooth, well-molded face. As she faced McCall, she was very much in charge, as if she handled men like him every day—which, was possible, since drifters often stopped for jobs or eats.

Surprised to see a woman, McCall blurted, "I'm looking for a man, ma'am."

"Well, I'm not." The brown eyes assessed him coolly. "What do you want?"

"Well, I came to see the boss about putting me up for the night."

"First, I'm the boss, and second—" He was still being assessed, and McCall had the peculiar feeling that he was a side beef hanging from a hook, awaiting approval, "Yes, I guess we can put you up."

"I'll pay."

"We don't collect pay at the Running B." was the tart remark. "We aren't that bad off yet. Hang your saddle on the corral, and eat with the boys."

McCall tipped his hat and drove Dogs to the corral. Now there was a lady who most likely tightened her own cinch straps. Pretty thing, too. The boss? Unusual in this country, especially when it came to ranching.

The boss of the Running B watched McCall as he strolled Dogs to the corral. That man was no ordinary drifter. His equipment was too good, and his style was different. Most drifters came hat in hand, but this man tipped his like a fellow who'd learned manners someplace. Most drifters slumped in the saddle, as if they were weary of the life they led, a life of wandering, a bit futile. This man sat straight in his saddle, and his eyes were bright with curiosity—plus another ingredient, anger. She had met an angry man, and a mystery.

That evening over biscuits and gravy in the mess hall, he learned her name was Lottie Branch. She ran the place alone because her father had died of the fever two years before. Her mother had been dead for longer than most could remember. Only the foreman had known her mother.

"I been with the spread fifteen years, ever since old man Branch started it," the foreman offered. He was a taciturn man, browned and wrinkled by the weather, a man who spoke carefully and commanded the respect of the toughest kind of worker in the world, the cowboy. McCall knew the type. More than any, or at least as much, they helped open the West with their knowledge of ranching. When he spoke, the others listened.

"No husband?" It was a personal question, but a common one in a part of the country where unmarried women Lottie's age were a wonder.

"Nope. Had a feller once, I think, but he disappeared somewheres—went to make his fortune in the Black Hills, they tell."

McCall changed the subject. You could ask questions about women like Lottie Branch, but not too many. One drop of water too much could make a five-gallon bucket overflow.

"I'd like to know," he said, addressing the men clinking silverware on the long table, "if any of you heard of two men, Blake and Scar." He described them.

There was a silence as jaws ground vittles, and McCall figured he wasn't going to get an answer.

Then a young man, no more than sixteen, said, "I think I saw 'em once over in Leadville."

McCall's voice brittled, like hard candy. "How long ago, son?"

"Oh," the youth scratched his head, "mebbe two months, somethin' like that."

"They's been some robberies and like that around here," put in another man, swallowing a huge slug of inky coffee, "an' they say a couple of fellers like you describe is head of the bunch."

"Recently?" McCall tensed.

"Nope, not too recent. They hit a few places then disappeared."

So! McCall didn't know if he was satisfied or not. He'd learned that Blake and Scar—all chances pointed to the gang leaders being them—were around, but nobody knew where they were now. Still, it was the most information he'd had of the two killers in some time. He'd have to reach Leadville.

That night, while Dogs dined on oats courtesy of the Running B, McCall lay awake in the bunkhouse. Back at his own spread, he often spent time in the bunkhouse, getting a kick out of the men swapping lies. He was at home in the cowboy's "castle," as they called the place. He listened to the snorts and snores of men asleep, and smelled the rank smell of sweaty bodies, and envied them. They knew where they were, and what was expected of them—an honest day's work for a day's pay. The bunkhouse wasn't much— cottonwood logs and a sod roof—but it was warm and dry, and the meals were good. And they had the companionship of each other. They lived in an isolated world out on the range, their own world in a way. They had all they needed at the ranch provided by the owner, in this case Lottie Branch. The ranch was their anchor. They were a happy bunch, and they shouted and whistled as they forked anxious broncs for the day's work.

Before leaving, McCall saw the girl. She was talking to the foreman, and he went to pay his respects.

"Take them out to the east range, Lon," she was saying. "Lots of new grass there."

"Yes ma'am." Lon nodded. "Think them cattle will fatten enough for a fall sale, I do believe, ma'am."

"We can use the money, Lon."

The foreman nodded, cast a look at McCall, then left, his work cut out.

"Thanks, Miss Branch," McCall said. "I'll be moving along."

"Need work?" The brown eyes reflected curiosity.

"No. Not now."

"What'd they do to you?"

McCall was surprised by the question. "Who do you mean?"

"Those two men, ah, Scar and somebody."

"How'd you know?"

But of course, McCall realized at once who the source was. Lon. Good foremen reported everything to the boss, particularly if the news was curious such as one man looking for two.

"They must have done something terrible." Lottie didn't linger on her question.

"Yes." McCall's voice became terrible. There was no change in the timbre, but a tightness that strung his voice like an off-key guitar.

The girl flushed and murmured, "I'm sorry. I didn't mean to pry."

"You have the right." McCall tipped his hat. "Thank you again for your kindness."

He turned Dogs to leave, when the girl's voice followed. "Will you come this way again?"

"I'm from down south, ma'am. Might be I'll reach the Running B on my way back, yes."

"When will that be?"

"After my business is finished."

"Oh." Men were leaving, their horses bucking out of morning orneriness. "Well, I'm going out with them today. See you." Her voice was suddenly serious. "Good luck. Be careful."

As McCall picked up the rutted trail that would eventually take him to Leadville, he felt strangely good. It was the girl's last words that elevated his spirits. He didn't know her, she didn't know him, and yet she was concerned. *Be careful*!

Nothing would come of her concern, of course. They would probably never meet again. Chances were his return trail would not converge on the Running B. This was big country.

Still, he missed a woman's concern. He missed his wife's concern, she of the golden hair and blue, loving eyes. He missed her waving goodbye in the morning. He missed her caring if he was wet or dry or worried, or in danger. He missed holding her to him, sharing his problems, or the good things by the fire at night. He missed a woman in his life, but it was too soon to think of any other. The memory of his wife, Belle, and sweet daughter, Katherine, lying in their blood on the cold ground, drove all thoughts of other women from his mind.

Yet the concern of Lottie Branch had been nice, and McCall felt good inside. He loved Belle and Kathy, oh, yes, with all his heart, and he was putting his life on the line for them. But it was good somebody like Lottie was concerned. She was a good one, that one. Belle would have liked her.

Chapter Four

Far back down the trail, at just about the place where the sun loses its daily battle with night, a man slogged along on his horse. His sharp mustaches glistened like stilettos in the clear, blue air, and his eyes were watchful.

Turk Siderack was not weary, but angry. He was angry with himself for his loyalty to his no-good brothers. Though he couldn't claim sainthood for himself, far from it, he felt himself to be better than a few cuts above his brothers. He went in for a more profitable aspect of crime: he worked alone. His brothers had worked with gangs—rustlings, stagecoach trimming, and the like. After he'd broken them in to the profits and losses of the Owl Hoot Trail, they'd deserted.

"They's safety in numbers," his brothers had told him, "and we aim t' git that safety."

Turk snorted in disgust. So where did that safety land them? At the quivering ends of hemp ropes, and the ropes, he'd bet, were probably not even new. They'd been hanged by gruesome tools used once before. Ach!

Yes, he worked alone. He made his own plans and carried them out. If they were successful, he could give himself credit; if they failed, he had only himself to blame. There was nobody else to bollix things. He was a robber, a highwayman, a hire-for-pay killer—any chore that might be offered a freelance outlaw, he took on. There was more profit, too, when a man worked alone—no need to split. And he liked flexibility and freedom. He also reasoned, many times, that he must be good, because he had a great deal of money in the bank to prove it.

He'd been on the trail of McCall for a month, not even knowing if he was taking the right direction, when his first clue came.

It happened in a town called Neb's Corner, in a bar called Neb's Golden Saloon. Apparently, he reasoned, this fellow, Neb, was an ambitious man.

He was having his favorite drink, rock and rye, and asking, as he did in every town, about McCall. All he could do was describe him, and he spoke, always, to the man who might be standing next to him.

The man next to him this time was a small fellow, with lines in his face so deep they threw shadows. He wore the garb of a professional cowboy—jeans, blue shirt, tall hat, and neckerchief. His feet were clad in leather boots with long pointed toes and high heels.

"Say," he muttered, after hearing Turk's description, "I do remember that man." He had a squeaky voice which grated, but Turk was suddenly very alert. "Yeah, he was in here about a few weeks ago, I guess, an' he was looking fer somebody, too."

"Oh?"

"Yeah, looking for a feller with a scar and another with a hot temper. I seen both of them, too, so I tolt him."

"Would you say those men were called Blake and Scar?"

The cowboy paused, then nodded. "Yeah, seems I did hear 'em jabberin' at each other and usin' them names. That's what I tolt that other feller, the one you lookin' fer." Eyes that had watched sky kiss earth at long distances for many years were shrewd. "You know them two?"

"Heard of 'em."

"Bad pair. I hear they got them a gang back East someplace."

"Where, man, where?"

"Dunno exactly. Mebbe, Wyoming or Dakota or Montan'."

Turk downed his drink and wiped his mustache on a sleeve. He bought the cowboy two drinks and left, his lips formed into a hard grin. Finally! McCall was still looking for Blake and Scar, so he too would hunt out Blake and Scar.

Back at the Running B, Lottie Branch was getting ready for winter. She'd seen to it her cattle were in the proper sections of the range, and had the wood hauled in— great loads of trees from riverbanks, where trees grew freely. The hay had been scythed and stacked, and winter horses selected for the small cadre of cowboys needed for the coming months.

She was satisfied. So far, she had held her own. She knew there'd been gossip in the country about a woman running a ranch alone. It wasn't done.

"Man's work," one fellow rancher told her bluntly. "You ought to get a husband, Lottie."

There was something about that general attitude that set Lottie's teeth on edge. She'd helped her father run the ranch ever since she'd been old enough to ride. She knew ranch work as well as the most thoroughbred of cowboys and ranchers. She'd done it all, from branding to butchering an occasional cow for the table—though, she admitted, she didn't care for the butchering end of it much.

There were enough remarks about ranching being "man's work" to make Lottie's ire rise to a high pitch. She had a good foreman to boss the men, she had bookkeeping sense, and she knew the cycles of cow-raising from spring to winter and back again. She knew how to run the ranch itself, how to keep the cooks happy, how to keep men happy. She set her jaw. She alone would operate the Running B.

Since her father died, there had been suitors. They were mainly young men from neighboring ranches, whose fathers urged them to marry a "good deal," not that Lottie wasn't worth having in her own right. Others were from Haystock, the shipping center ten miles north. They were all nice young men, courteous, who took her on picnics and to dances in town. And they were all eager to know about the ranch. How many cattle? How much acreage? Etcetera.

Lottie fielded them all, knowing exactly what they wanted. She led them down the trail of expectancy, enjoying their company for a time, then dumped them without ceremony. She admitted that what she did was probably "not nice," but then, had they been "nice"? They were belled cats as far as she was concerned, and she was one mouse that would not serve as dinner.

There had been one man a boss from the Bar X, who showed promise. James P. Coop. But he turned out to be a gambler, a drinker, and, Lottie suspected, had too much romance in him for one woman to handle. Because she liked him, she was, more sparing of his feelings than the others when she indicated his efforts were futile.

"You're nice, Jim," she said, "and competent, I know that, and maybe we could be happy. But you know, and I know, that you'll never settle down. You have free habits, and those habits are fun for you, and it is hard to break fun habits. I won't put you in a position where you'll be unhappy."

"What do you mean?" asked James B. Coop.

"I mean goodbye, Jim."

And he disappeared into the jaws of the great country surrounding them. Lottie never did hear what happened to him.

There were times when she was lonely. She missed her father; she'd liked the security he gave. He had been like a forest protecting its sapling. She wondered, sometimes, if she ever would marry. Nobody so far had measured up. She was aware, too, that a young woman didn't dare be too precious with her preferences in a country that didn't have many to choose from. But she was only twenty-four; there was time.

In spite of discouragement in romance, she did find herself thinking of that fellow who'd spent the night a few weeks before. McCall. There was nothing particularly im-

pressionable about him—except his good
looks, strength, and quiet, courtly manner.
Lottie smiled at this. Oh no, nothing! Yet
others who had come with Cupid in their
hearts had been as handsome. There was
more to McCall, though. His deep anger
intrigued her. It was an anger born of great
pain. The fire in his eyes excited her,
though the fire was not for her. It was the
fire of vengeance. Lottie knew it when she
saw it, because she'd been involved in
range wars and Indian attacks back in ear-
lier times, and she saw that same fire in the
eyes of survivors. What had happened to
him? She saw, also, more than the anger.
She saw a damaged man, a man intent on
giving death to others unknown to her, and
that drive would destroy him if it was not
fulfilled. He would live with the destruction
in his soul forever, and he would become
the victim. For Lottie had seen that, too.
When great hate went unavenged, those
who carried the hate became embittered
and looked upon life with yellow eyes.
Their souls turned to rawhide.

Lottie Branch found herself wanting that
not to happen to McCall, and she wondered
why she thought of him at all—especially

in such depth. Who was this man, this *real*
man, after?

The men McCall were after were in
Leadville.

"We'll go after that stage in the morning," Blake was saying. "The Army payroll
is on it."

"We don't want to monkey with Army
money," Scar objected.

"We've already gone over this." Blake
was impatient. "I told you, we'll kill 'em
all, and leave no witnesses." His eyes glit-
tered with remembrance. "You know how
I am about that."

Scar nodded. He grinned. "Yeah. We
should have got them folks at that last stage
back in Indian Country."

"No time, if you recall? Them troopers
was comin'!"

"Yeah. Too bad. Them dudes needed
killin', far I was concerned, and them
women . . . well." He clapped his hands together and laughed coarsely.

"You two goin' t' settle this?" a third
voice chimed in.

Blake and Scar had kept to their aim and
added more men to form a gang. There
were an additional five now, all with rec-
ords.

"None of them," Blake told Scar with satisfaction, "a mother would want to call 'son.' "

"Yeah," Blake told the speaker, "we get that stage."

"Good enough," another voice ventured, a hard, impersonal voice. "We was beginning to wonder if we'd joined with the right ones. You kep' arguin'. You don't argue 'bout these things—you agree, or they don't work."

Blake's pistol was out of its holster in a blink.

"You don't like it, Carter, you kin beat it. But," he grinned with malice, "since you know too much, I doubt you'll git far." He cocked his pistol and aimed at the other man's forehead. "I like to aim," he said, "to make sure."

"Hey!" squawked Carter, "you don't need t' git so hot, Blake. We got a right to ast questions, you know."

"Not when I'm running things. You-all remember that. Me an' Scar run things, but, naturally, we got to discuss them a bit. See?" His eyes bored into Carter like .45 slugs. "That satisfy you, Carter?"

And Carter, a killer of men, and once a leader of his own gang of cutthroats, preying mainly on the Oregon Trail wagon trains, nodded. He was pale, knowing he'd come just a finger squeeze from meeting the emptiness of eternity.

Blake pulled a soiled map from a jacket so dirty it could have been planted with parsnips. He unfolded the map, and pointed to a spot he'd marked with an "X."

"The wagon should pass here at about noon tomorrow, according to what I heard."

"Hope you heard right," muttered some-body, not Carter.

"You can be sure of it!" snapped Blake. "I got it from a bluebelly at the fort."

Like most towns in the Plains country, Leadville was first a fort, then a town—the town springing up a mile or so away, to serve the fort. Forts offered security from Indians and bandits, and any town growing in the fort's protective reach survived. It drew people and grew, and Leadville was now a jumping off place for Laramie and the Dakota Black Hills.

It was evident that Blake had paid for his information, and that was good enough for the rest. Blake, on the other hand, realized that no matter how tough and ruthless he was, he would lose the gang if his plans went wrong. He might also lose his own life, since none of the new members were beyond shooting him out of pure cussedness. They didn't know him as a leader yet. He'd brought them together on a jawbone only; Blake was a persuasive speaker. But like a snowman, he was vulnerable to heat, and he was cunning enough to realize that. A lot depended on tomorrow's venture, if he and Scar were to keep the gang and profit from it.

The next day arrived with birdsong. The gang had camped some miles from Leadville, pretending to the casual observer in town that they were leaving for points south, maybe Abilene. It was a great day to be alive. Aside from birdsong, there was a cool wind that would condition the sun to a man's liking, and the great sky above was so blue that even Carter remarked, "Looks like my mother's eye."

That brought a laugh, even a smile from Blake. They rode in good spirits to the point marked "X" on the map, and were satisfied to find the place well stocked with huge boulders. They parked behind boulders, hidden from sight, and waited.

At eleven in the morning, the Army wagon could be heard approaching. It jingled and jangled and squeaked, sending out the message that this wagon feared nothing.

"Sounds like a moving blacksmith shop," muttered one of the gang, which brought a rumble of low-keyed laughter.

"You-all ready?" hissed Blake, no longer in a mood for humor.

Nods greeted his question.

"All right, now remember—no survivors."

The men readied their weapons. They were edgy, but the thought of killing didn't bother them. They were professionals in this game and knew exactly the value of Blake's deadliness, even approved it. But like actors about to go onstage, no matter how seasoned, they were nervous.

The wagon drove into view. It was a freighter of large dimensions, hauled by a double span of four horses. Two troopers were in the driver's seat, one holding reins, the other a carbine. Four troopers flanked the wagon itself, and two brought up the rear. There were eight men attending the pay wagon. They were tough men, browned by weather, eyes dark with what they'd seen in the current Indian uprisings. They rode without fear.

Blake quickly assigned a blue-coated target to each of his men.

"There'll be one left," he whispered, and his voice was strangely exuberant. "I'll get him, too. Just be sure you get yours. Fire when I give the signal."

The troopers drew abreast, no more than fifty feet from the hidden outlaws. At that point, Blake dropped his hand, and seven rifles sent echoes that caused the blue sky to shiver and birdsong to cease.

Seven troopers fell in death, their horses galloping aimlessly. The shocked driver of the wagon drew to a halt. Blake confronted him, and, smiling, gave him a bullet hole squarely between the eyes. Somebody grabbed the reins to keep the frightened team from running. Somebody else threw off two boxes, and still others tied them to the back of a packhorse, brought along for the purpose.

Two of the gang started to strip the dead soldiers of their guns. Blake immediately stopped it.

"Nothing will be taken except the money in those boxes," he ordered sharply. "We don't want to carry giveaway messages with us, understood?"

The two nodded sullenly, but one muttered, "We ought ter at least git what cash they got on 'em. We kin spend that and they ain't nobody goin' t' know."

Blake saw the sense to that, so the soldiers were robbed, and the gang left with their loot. The eight soldiers were left to stare at the sun with dead eyes.

Thereafter in the country, a fearsome gang terrorized the trails. The gang became known as the "Kill 'em Alls," because nobody was ever left alive. Nobody knew what the murderers looked like, because there were no descriptions.

But McCall had a hunch, and he hunted for the gang. Whenever a new atrocity had been committed by the Kill 'em Alls, he was there soon after, asking questions. But he could never learn anything conclusive. He hung on. Sometime, somewhere, there would be a mistake. It was bound to happen, and then he would be able to act.

Far to the rear, Turk Siderack thought the same, for he, too, knew of the gang. He was thinking about that as he pulled into Lottie Branch's Running B.

Chapter Five

As McCall neared Leadville, he began to formulate a more definite plan for getting Blake and Scar. So far he had trusted to a sort of deadly lottery. Guess the right trail and maybe—bang!—he'd win a target.

That wasn't enough. He'd wandered a thousand miles or more looking for the pair, but they evaded him. They were like wet snakes in wet hands, slippery. The odd thing was, their successful evasion was accidental. They had no notion, so far as he knew, that he was after them. Coincidence was playing too large a part in his life. That would have to change.

There was another way. What was the

saying—birds of a feather flock together? Well, then, he'd become a bird. He let his beard grow. It was the first time he'd grown a beard, and he was bemused by its appearance. He had dark hair, but his beard was so red that the contrast startled him. Every time he looked in the tin mirror he carried in his saddlebag, he was reminded of some savage creature like Captain Kidd of pirate fame, maybe, or a half-wild mountain man. The beard would do.

His mustache was also a luxuriant growth, and also red. He captured the habit of twirling it regularly, and along with the twirling developed a harsh laugh. He changed the sound of his voice to a guttural series of grunts and monosyllables, and looked on the world with narrowed eyes. The anger in them was real enough, but all the rest was an act.

When he reached Leadville, he could pass for anybody's outlaw, or at least a man of ill will. He lodged Dogs at a hostelry and moseyed uptown to the first bar. He put his two-drink limit aside and downed several shots noisily, with the belligerence of a very thirsty steer. He displayed his money carelessly in an easy-come-easy-go fashion, though not all of it. A good portion he left in his room. After all, he was not a real bad man, and there might be some around who would, and could, lift his riches as easily as lifting a hooked trout from a stream. He wanted a reserve in case that happened.

Leadville was a mining boomtown. Characters of all kinds roamed the streets in giddy bands. Mountain men from the Rockies, cowboys from Texas, horse soldiers from Laramie, infantry from Benson, gamblers, dance hall women, businessmen in tall, silk hats, honest men, ambitious men and women, dullards and sharpies mingled like yeasted bread dough, and swelled in numbers by the day.

It was a noisy assemblage. Shouts, oaths, and even prayers mingled in a babble of excited talk about new gold strikes in the "Blacks." McCall fit in well with his red beard, black hair, and trail-roughed clothing. He noted that dress was a peculiarly individual matter—it all depended on what the individual could get. There were those who paraded in tailor-made suits and fedoras; those whose frames were clad in buckskin, signifying they'd been long alive among the crinkled hills of the upper Plains country. Others, much like McCall, wore the ordinary store-bought clothing available—Levi trousers, hickory-striped shirts, high boots, and warm jackets.

A few men were trailed by Indian women and several children. They were hard-faced, sharp-eyed men, men nobody fooled with. They lived with the danger of the wilderness and unfriendly Indians and whites on a daily basis, and did not know about the more gentle aspects of life. They were curt and strangely subdued. So many people made them uneasy, for they were accustomed to great silences. Yet they, too, needed to trade goods in town, and chanced the aggravation to get what they wanted.

McCall put step number one of his plan into action. With his limit of two drinks set aside, he hoisted a few more, showing money but talking little. He deliberately set himself into the character of one who has money to burn yet keeps to himself. His eyes were steely, and his lips, under the massive red beard, thinned into rawhide. He scanned the bar crowd closely, watchful, waiting for the right moment.

It came after his fourth drink—after he'd decided that four were enough, and he switched to beer. Two tough men pushed through the door and found a table in a far corner. They ordered a bottle and dug out a pack of cards. They said little as they played a two-handed game, intent on the outcome. McCall noted that they sat with their backs to the wall, and every time somebody entered, they gave him a full survey, like cats eyeing a chicken.

They would do.

McCall sauntered over. "What you playing?" he asked.

"Just a game," said one, a man with narrow eyes.

"Mind if I join in?"

"Yes, we mind," said the other, a man with a large wart on the side of his nose.

"Well, say," McCall said, raising his voice, "that ain't very friendly."

Narrow eyes looked him over. "Beat it."

McCall wasn't about to leave. He was getting just what he wanted—an entry into a world beyond the restrictions of law.

"What's the matter, you men afraid of a little honest poker?"

"Shut up," advised Wart Nose.

"I want in that game."

By now, patrons of bar were looking, which was fine with McCall. Everything was falling into place. His plan was far-fetched, yet it was the only one he had. A man simply didn't go around asking who was an outlaw. He was apt to end up with lead poisoning, or knifed like a Thanksgiving turkey.

Narrow Eyes stood up. "We don't want you here."

His hand hovered near his pistol. He knew when a man was picking a deliberate fight, and the fellow in the red beard was doing just that—though it was mystifying. He and his companion had made enemies, sure, but Narrow Eyes could not recall this giant.

"You yellow?" demanded McCall in his most belligerent voice.

Narrow Eyes' hand flicked, but McCall was waiting and edged him out on the draw. The two pistols roared. The .45 slug from Narrow Eyes' gun splintered the floor. That was just before the lead from McCall's pistol splattered his weapon into pieces.

Narrow Eyes roared with the sting as his Colt disintegrated. Wart Nose started for his own equalizer, but McCall coolly calmed him down with a wave of his smoking barrel.

"Don't," he ordered harshly. "Next time I won't be so easy."

"All's we was doin' was having a drink and a little cards," yelled Narrow Eyes, "an' you come bustin' in. By dang, mister, I aim t' git you, after a doctor sees my hand." He gazed at the injured appendage. "She's so numb, fire would make 'er laugh."

McCall nodded and pointed to the door. "You're welcome to leave. All's I wanted was a friendly game." He reached in a pocket and withdrew a sheaf of golden back currency. "You might have had a good time with me."

There were murmurs in the crowd. For one thing, golden backs were not seen often, and they meant big money. For another, nobody showed how much money he had—not in Leadville. That was an advertisement for sleepy time, as prescribed by a blow to the back of the head after dark.

The two tough-looking gents departed. The excitement over, the crowd drifted back to former amusements, and McCall returned to the bar. All right: he had advertised that he was a hard case, that he was a good shot, and that he had money. Two things might happen now. One, somebody—a recruiter—could sound him out, or two, he might be the target of men who saw his bankroll. Either way, it meant entry into a gang, though the first possibility was best.

As he was finishing his beer, he watched a small person ease from the bar. He had ordered his third beer and was about to call it quits for the better effects of a restaurant, when the small person returned. He sidled up to the bar and ordered.

"Seen you with that gun," he remarked casually.

"Yeah," said McCall, pretending no particular interest. The stained walls of the place seemed much more intriguing.

"Seen you with that money, too," was the follow up remark.

"Better talk about something else," McCall said gently, but with deadly meaning.

"You don't seem to scare."

"What, of those two gents? Nah!" He snorted his disgust. "I've seen tougher sheep."

The small man watched him with close-set eyes. He nodded and sipped his refreshment.

"They," he said, "are two of the worst mountebanks this side of the Mississippi.

They used to belong to the Kill 'em All gang."

McCall shrugged. "I heard of that bunch. Ain't much, I don't think. Used to run with the James boys myself."

The small man's eyes widened. "I knew there was something about you," he murmured. "All that money and good shootin'." He paused. "My name is Shook Smith, they call me Shooky." He stuck out a hand. "Glad to meet you."

McCall took the extended hand, then dropped it. "Pleased, Shooky."

There was a silence. Then Shooky said confidentially, as if he were planning a prison escape, "You still interested?"

"Interested in what?"

"Well, a little extra money, for one thing."

McCall grunted and continued the nonchalance, but he was keyed to a high pitch, an eagle about to dive for its quarry. "I got enough money, you seen that."

The other's face dropped a bit.

"But," McCall went on, "I could always use more, sure. What you got in mind?"

"I'd like you to meet some fellers."

"What are you, some kind of a scout?"

Shooky grinned. "You could say that."

McCall nodded. "Figured that. The James boys scouted me the same way." He finished his beer. "Where and when do I meet these gentlemen?"

"Tonight at eight. They'll be at the Clover." Shooky mentioned another bar down the street. "That's headquarters."

McCall nodded, and without another word, left. He had rented a hotel room and returned quickly, with perhaps more animation than ordinarily. He felt something in the pit of his stomach and realized it was excitement. His whole body was tense. Would he be meeting with Blake and Scar? After all this time, all these miles, would he come face to face with the men who killed his wife and daughter, the men who wiped out his life?

He checked his Colt to see it was properly loaded, all six chambers filled with deadly .45 lead slugs. He tested his holster for a fast draw. The holster was slick, and the heavy weapon slipped without hindrance from its nest. He paced the floor, and when he tired of that, he went to see that Dogs was getting proper care. Dogs was in good hands. The man in charge had curried him, fed him oats, and now he slept with three feet on the floor of the stable, the left front foot cocked at an angle.

"Lucky nag," muttered McCall. "Nothing bothers you as long as you got oats, right?"

Dogs woke and turned his head. He seemed to wink at McCall, gave a gentle whinny, and returned to his occupation— sleeping. McCall patted the well-muscled rump and grinned. "You bum, you," he said quietly. "You and I, we've come a long way."

The time dragged. There was a rope on time, holding it back. There was a trap on time's foot, a snare. Time had fallen into a pit, and couldn't get out. Time dragged.

By seven in the evening, though, McCall had gotten over the jitters. His head was clear, and he demolished a sizeable steak dinner. By seven in the evening, he was calm again. The tightness in his stomach was still there, but modified. It was the edge of a lake touching shore, letting him know that water, perhaps deep water, waited if he left shore. He chose to leave.

At eight he entered the Clover. The place was alive with evening customers, enjoying a drink and some piano music. The man at the keyboard wore a derby hat and sleeve bands, and he played with a concentration that would have put a mathematician to shame.

McCall edged through the happy throng looking for—he didn't know just what. Then, without warning, Shooky took him by the arm.

"Come with me."

He led the way to a back room. There was a single lamp in the room, and McCall guessed it was deliberately shadowed so he could be seen, but not see. Several figures were sitting at a round table.

"Sit down," said one of the figures, but McCall remained on his feet.

"I said sit down," repeated the voice.

"I choose to stand."

"Suit yourself."

This was followed by a silence, and McCall felt eyes studying him. They were hard eyes, wolfish, hunter eyes, eyes that were without the preamble of friendliness.

Another voice: "Seems you're pretty young to have traveled with the James boys."

"I was a kid then."

"What'd you say your name was?"

"I didn't say."

"We'd like t' know."

McCall took the lead now, pushing back. "Why am I here?" he demanded.

"I think you know," returned the first voice.

"I know nothing."

"What's your name—Shooky, you know it?"

"No," said that individual. "He ain't no friend."

McCall thought quickly. "Name is Pitt," he said.

There was a stir, among the figures, a whispered conference. Then the first voice hardened. "I don't know anybody named Pitt."

McCall matched the other's tone. "Neither do I."

That brought a dry chuckle. "Yeah, well, mebbe you better learn it."

McCall said nothing.

One of the shadows spoke. "If you was with the James boys, what you know about Ottersville?"

McCall thanked his stars for that one. Everybody in the West knew about the train robbery at Ottersville. There was a hundred-thousand-dollar haul in that one.

"I got my share," he said.

"Then what?"

"We hit a bank in Northfield and got shot up bad. Only Jesse and Frank and me got away. I quit after that. Went on my own."

There was another stir among the shadows, and McCall heard approving sounds. So far he passed inspection.

"All right," came the first voice. "Be here at dawn tomorrow morning. I mean early, man. We'll see what happens. Shooky, take him out."

He was led out, and Shooky returned to the room. McCall was both elated and alarmed. Were the men in that room members of the Kill 'em All gang? And what was tomorrow all about? Well, at least, he was sure he had an inside track with the bad element of the country—whoever the gang. And that was important. Tomorrow would bring—whatever!

Chapter Six

Lottie Branch watched as the bulldog of a man approached. As he drew closer, she was fascinated by the mustache. Many men grew them in the country, but they were ragged, unkempt things. The men called them soup strainers, but those on the stranger spun straight out on either side. They were twirled tight, probably kept tight by some kind of wax, and they looked for all the world like the mustaches of Prussian officers. Lottie was a great reader, and she'd seen pictures.

There was something about the rider that was unsettling to Lottie. She couldn't figure it out. It was like looking at a painting she didn't understand. The picture itself was harmless enough, but an intangible quality jarred her senses. She hadn't even spoken to the rider yet, but sensed danger. Perhaps it was the way he rode his horse, sort of hunched forward in a seeking position. Perhaps it was the stern, hard face of the man. Something.

She was, therefore, surprised when the rider spoke. His voice was soft and pleasant.

"Howdy, Miss," said the bulldog, "I'm hungry and looking for a meal. Can I invade your mess hall?"

"Of course."

"Cooky won't kill me? It's only three in the afternoon."

Lottie reconsidered quickly. It was the habit of most ranch cooks to take time off in the afternoon. They were up at five in the morning and worked till after the noon meal; then they took a recess until about four. Cooks were very jealous of that time off, and they guarded it like the proverbial dog in the manger. It was a time in which they rested, or performed personal chores. It was always dangerous to intrude.

The girl glanced around the yard. Lon, the foreman, was supervising barn repair with several men. With them near, she felt safe, so she said, "Come into the ranch house, then. I'll fix you a sandwich."

This was something Lottie seldom did—feed strangers in her home—but she was curious about this stranger, who spoke softly but bore himself like a bomb about to explode. She sensed the tension in the man, as easily as she might feel heat from the kitchen range.

Turk Siderack murmured a soft thank-you and dismounted. He hitched his horse to the rail and followed Lottie inside. He doffed his broad-brimmed hat and hung it on a rack near the entry. Lottie quickly made a beef sandwich and poured a cup of coffee. She noted that the stranger kept glancing out the window, eyes alert and, so it seemed to the girl, hopeful.

"If you're looking for work," she said by way of opening conversation, "I'm afraid the Running B is laying men off. It's September, and we keep only a few men over winter."

The stranger, hunched over the table in the same way he hunched forward on his horse, shook his head. He was a gargoyle of a man, thought Lottie, ugly but strong, very powerful. She would hate to have him as an enemy. But when he responded to her statement, she was, once again, surprised by the soft voice.

"No, ma'am, I'm not looking for work. By the way"—he smiled so broadly that even the ice-pick mustaches curved up—" forgive my manners. I'm Turk Siderack."

Lottie was slightly jarred by Turk's yellowed teeth. Somehow she expected to see shiny white ivories from a mouth that spoke so gently.

In response to the expectant look in the watchful eyes, she said, "I'm Lottie Branch. I run this spread."

"Unusual work for a woman."

"I was raised to it." Lottie felt a little heat. Here was typical male condescension. "There are many women in this part of the country who know the cattle business."

Turk laughed, and the sound was not harsh, but like his voice, soft and pleasing. "I beg your pardon, ma'am. I didn't mean to imply you couldn't. Come to think of it, women have quite a bit to say where I come from."

"Are you from far off?" Lottie asked.

"Oh, a long way."

"Texas, judging from your drawl."

For the briefest of moments, Turk's eyes

flashed with resentment, but the moment passed, and he remained pleasant.

"I don't generally tell where I'm from," he said smoothly. "Not that it matters. Nobody is looking for me—such as the law. It's just a matter of, ah, personal policy."

"Sorry. I didn't mean to intrude."

Lottie was slightly embarrassed. In her great curiosity about this unusual man, she had overstepped the courtesy of the range. One never asked personal questions or made judgments, as she just had.

"That's all right, but since we've opened the conversation some, there is a question I'd like to ask."

Lottie smiled. "I'd be obliged to answer."

"Can you tell me if a man named McCall has been by?"

Startled, Lottie uttered a word that she regretted immediately. "Yes."

Turk leaned forward, his eyes glowing like hot coals in the fireplace. "I'm looking for him," he said in the same pleasant voice. "Could you tell me which way he headed?"

The girl hesitated, then lied, "I don't really know."

"Did he go to Leadville or the Dakotas?"

"He didn't say. He just stayed overnight, then left. I hardly spoke to him."

The girl realized that she was, suddenly, fighting the man opposite her. That he was jabbing verbally, trying to gouge information that was very important to him. This dangerous man, this creature who spoke so pleasantly, smiled so nicely, but bore a resemblance to a mustached gargoyle, wanted information that would put McCall in danger. This Turk Siderack hadn't come all the way from Texas on a joyride. Lottie Branch had met all kinds of men in her life on the Plains, many of them bad men, and many of them not bearing the appearance of evil in the slightest. As a young girl in her teens, she had met Billy the Kid, probably the most wanted outlaw in the West. He boldly came to a dance in Haystock and was most courteous to all. From that experience, she had learned that manners do not tell the story.

"Do you know," said Turk, his voice no longer soft, "that man killed my two brothers?"

"McCall?" Lottie's memory conjured up the tall man who had come into her life, and in the cup of that memory, she remembered no evil. McCall was not a killer. If the brothers had been slain by him, there must have been good reason.

"If he did," she said, "there must have been good reason."

"Reason?" Turk Siderack's suppressed anger burst forth like a volcanic eruption. "He saw to it my brothers were hanged for something they didn't do. Then he ran off, before the law could get him." Turk's face was almost purple with rage. "The law wouldn't chase him, but I am. I've come all the way from Texas, little lady, to get him, and now I want to know, where is he?"

Turk, all veneer of the gentleman dissolved, banged a giant fist on the table with such violence that the dishes jumped, and a saucer fell to the floor. It made a loud, splintering crash.

"I have no idea where he is. Why would he tell me where he was going if he is wanted by the law?"

Turk's eyes blazed a peculiar yellow, a color almost matching his teeth.

"You'll tell me or . . ."

"Or what?" came a voice from the door.

Lon stood there, his pistol out. He was flanked by two of his men.

Turk turned on them savagely, and for a

moment, Lottie thought he was going for his gun. A clock ticked away the seconds on a shelf, and the wood stove, banked for daytime use, sputtered in the silence. Then Turk's manner changed abruptly.

"Oh, I say, now." He was smooth. "I don't want trouble here, Miss Branch."

He shoved past Lon and his men, and retrieved his hat from the rack. Lottie watched him, not moving, grateful that Lon had come; grateful for her foreman who probably from the start had kept an ear open.

"I'll be going now," said Turk, once again the gentleman, "but I did learn something: he's around this part of country." Then, very deliberately, he said 'I don't know what he means to you, Miss, but," a terrible smile revealed the repulsive yellow teeth, "I am going to kill him."

With that he mounted his horse and left.

Lon glanced at Lottie while shoving his weapon back into its holster. "You all right?"

"Yes, Lon. I'm fine."

"Who was he?"

"A man named Turk Siderack."

Lon thought a minute. Then his face lit up. "Siderack? Seems I heard of him when I was down in Texas. Not a nice feller, ma'am." Lon was stern. "Please don't invite strangers to your kitchen, Miss Branch. The boys and I won't always be around, you know?"

Lottie nodded. Lon always spoke formally to her, though she'd known him from childhood. Lon, though not old, assumed a fatherly interest in her. He nodded and turned to go. Then he paused. "What did he want you to tell him?"

"Oh, nothing."

"Must have been something, if you'll excuse the contradiction, ma'am. He was mad as a rattler in water."

"Well." Lottie hesitated, then saw no harm in telling. "He wanted to know where McCall was."

Lon registered surprise. "McCall? You mean that tall gent who was here a few weeks ago?"

"The same."

"But why?"

"Well—seems McCall killed two of his brothers—saw to it they were hung, anyway. Siderack says they were innocent."

"Yeah." Lon was cynical. "They all are." It was his turn to hesitate, but only for a second. "Did you tell him?"

"No."

Lon smiled, and in the smile was a knowledge of the human heart. "You sort of cotton to McCall, Miss Branch?"

"Of course not! I only knew him a day or two."

"Ma'am, excuse me, but it don't take long sometimes."

Lottie blushed. "All right," she said, laughing, "that'll be enough, Lon. What are you, Cupid? Go to work."

The men started to leave when Lottie stopped them. "No, for what you did, take the day off, I feel I owe you much, Lon."

The men departed on feet a bit more swift than before Lottie gave them time off. Payday hadn't been too long ago, and they still had money in their pockets. Haystock craved their company.

Lottie poured a cup of coffee for herself and sat at the kitchen table. She could see out the window on to endless miles of plains. As one cowboy put it, there was miles and miles of miles and miles. Somewhere out there was a man named McCall, and there was another named Turk Siderack, who in all probability meant to kill him. It was a matter of vengeance.

Could she do anything to warn McCall? Even before she finished that thought, she realized there was nothing she could do. McCall could be anyplace—Leadville, the Dakotas, Montana, anyplace in his own quest. He'd had the time over a period of several weeks to reach far places. He was lost to her, as surely as if he'd sunk into an ocean.

Then she mused on something else. Had Lon been closer to the truth than even she knew? With Lon, his statement about her "cottoning" to the tall man had been, in part at least, banter. He was close enough to her that he could tease her—and he did. Lottie had come to the conclusion that he wanted her safely married. Not that he didn't admire her independence and ability. It was just the father instinct in him. Every girl should get married and be safe.

She had thought of McCall often and wondered what he was up to. She wondered if she'd ever see him again—and was both embarrassed and amused by her concern. After all, she had only known him for that short time, And, yet, the time they had was more vivid to her than any she'd spent with a man before. Surely, surely, she couldn't be in love on so short a notice.

She thought about Turk, the bulldog man with the queer mustache, and felt him to be a tenacious type, a man who would stick to his goals no matter now many obstacles. And she'd given him a clue that McCall was in the nearby country! She had done so innocently, but nevertheless, she had put McCall's life in jeopardy.

At that moment, Lottie Branch didn't like herself very much. She stifled an impulse to go after the man, Siderack, and tell him she'd been lying. He'd never believe her. She also stifled an impulse to ride after him with a gun. That was silly—though one sure way of keeping a man she loved alive.

Life could get complicated. She settled the questions by going to work. Men were cutting more wood for winter down by the Platte. She went to help them. Hard work was a great way to forget troubles.

Nearly out of sight of the Running B, a bleep on the horizon, Turk pushed his horse toward Haystock. He would pause there for food and drink, then head for Leadville. The man he would kill might be there. Maybe not, but the gap was closing. Turk allowed a smile. The time was near.

He was still angry at himself for getting into the present situation. He should have been back in his own part of world. There was money to be made there, and that money was getting by—lots of pilgrims coming in, waiting for a holdup man to relieve them of the worry of money and jewels. There were many stages passing through without his personal attention. There were men to be killed upon order of others with plenty of remuneration. He was missing all that because of family!

Well, once this was over, the family honor avenged, he'd be heading home himself, and never again, would he commit to such a quest. Never again, would he have family honor to sustain. He was the last of the bunch. There were no more. His parents were dead, his brothers had been jerked into heaven, and he was the last.

Except . . . Turk smiled his great yellow-toothed smile . . . he did sort of like that little lady back at the Running B. Perhaps a little oil on the squeak he had made would smooth things out a bit?

It was a thought.

Chapter Seven

When McCall arrived at the Clover, the others were waiting.

"About time," growled one.

McCall recognized the voice as belonging to one of yesterday's speakers. He was a gaunt man, with slitted eyes and mouth. His face was without visible signs of emotion, a face devoid of compassion, a face fashioned and hardened by crime.

McCall quickly scanned the others. None bore a scar. None bore a sullen pudginess around the lips, a pout that told of chronic anger—the anger he'd heard Blake carried.

"Who," he asked, "leads this bunch?"

"I do," said the man with slitted eyes. "You can call me—Wolf."

There was a dry rustle of laughter at this, and McCall realized the name he got was phony. He didn't ask about names or who was who in the gang again. He was being tested, and until he proved himself, there would be no confidences. He did see Shooky, but the man kept to himself, and McCall didn't force the acquaintanceship.

He was disappointed. He had hoped to see Blake and Scar. He realized, however, from past experience, that even if he did see a pair that anwered the description of those he wanted, he couldn't be sure they were the right men. It would be necessary to somehow get confessions from them, some kind of bedrock admission they were the ones who killed his wife and daughter. And, there was this—Blake and Scar might not be in this bunch at all. They weren't present, and shouldn't they be when business was being conducted? Wolf seemed to be in charge.

The gang rode single file down the narrow road. There was little talk, and most of it about mundane matters, such as it was a hot day, and another was thirsty, and another about girls in Leadville. Nothing was said about what was going to happen, what this mission was about. They passed stage-coaches without comment, though McCall did note that the man riding shotgun sat straight up and the hammers on his 10-gauge were cocked.

Where was the goal? Or what was it? McCall was as certain as coming winter that a robbery was going to take place—but who?

When the sun had reached a point in the blue oven above where it was hot enough to bring sweat, Wolf raised a hand. The group stopped. McCall was puzzled. They seemed to be nowhere. There were hills nearby, and at the foot of the hills was a stream. The stream rippled noisily, causing faint echoes in the draws and cracks of the hills. Crows rasped, and clung to cotton-woods on the banks for shade.

"They should be along," was all Wolf said. "We'll hit the stream and wait."

The horses drank, men filled canteens, and McCall soaked his neckerchief, then wrapped it loosely around his neck. Who was expected? Another part of the gang—the leaders, perhaps?

He found himself fidgety inside, but was

careful not to show it. He lolled easily under a tree, hat tilted over his eyes. Nobody spoke to him. In fact, there was still little conversation, until one man said suddenly, "I wonder what they got this time?"

"Shut your mouth," growled Wolf, nodding at McCall. "We'll know soon enough."

The other lapsed into a sullen quiet.

They hadn't long to wait before four horsemen galloped into view. They followed the rutted trail, and when they saw McCall's band, cut over. Wolf, who had been shading himself at the side of a boulder, rose to greet them. The rest followed suit. A well-disciplined group, thought McCall. Was the discipline based on respect or fear?

The horsemen drew abreast, and McCall froze. His spine was ice. One of the men wore a vivid scar on his face, reaching from under his left eye to his chin. Another barked orders, but he was different from the killer that McCall had pictured. This was no pudgy-faced, sullen, trigger-happy murderer. This man was lean and hawk-faced, with slitted eyes that took in everything at a glance.

"We'll hit the Easton bank at midnight,"

he said crisply. Then his eyes flicked to McCall. "Who is this?" he demanded.

"New blood," said Wolf. "You said we needed more men if we were going to expand business. Shooky found him."

The hawk face split McCall's own features like an axe.

"How do we know about him?" he thundered. "Any proof about him, Shooky?"

"He was with the James boys, Blake."

Blake! McCall's tension mounted. So here they were at last, the two men who had killed his wife and daughter. Here they were, and all he had to do was shoot them. There was one obvious fault with that. One blast from his pistol would bring a dozen more from the gang. He'd be dead before he hit the ground.

And there was still another obstacle. He had heard these two were the killers, and he had followed their trail all the way from Texas, but he had no absolute proof they had done it. Nothing to go on save the word of the Siderack brothers, who, for reasons of their own, might want vengeance. Blake and Scar were a pair who could bring that wish from many. McCall didn't doubt that.

Blake intruded into McCall's thoughts

with a sharp laugh. "He says that, Shooky, but what proof you got?"

"He was at Ottersville, Blake."

"Anybody could know about that— that's history. Any liar could say he was in on it."

Those words played right into McCall's hand. His pistol was out in a flash.

"You calling me a liar?" he asked in a baritone that made antelope a mile away pause.

Blake studied him. The keen, cruel eyes looked him over and seemed to read his very soul. Evil was searching the bedrock of his being.

"You would," Blake said finally, "shoot me, when you know my men would cut you down?"

"Don't call me a liar." McCall turned contemptuous eyes on the others. "I'd get a couple first."

Blake nodded, and the nod brought evident relief to the gang. They stirred from frozen positions.

"He took on the McNulty boys." Shooky reinforced his argument. "I saw 'im do it. Took 'em on bold as brass. You know how they was when they ran with us."

"You talk too much," Blake said bluntly,

but he eyed McCall with new interest. "Put your gun away. What'd you say your name was?"

McCall nested his .45 back in its holster. "I didn't say."

"It's Pitt," interjected Shooky.

"Pitt?"

"Good as any," said McCall.

"Yeah. All right, we'll give you a try."

McCall came to an important point swiftly. "And you are Blake and Scar?"

Blake scowled. "We didn't say."

"Listen—I want in with the right bunch. I don't have time for beginners. This is the Kill 'em All gang, right?"

"We didn't say," growled Blake. "Don't get too inquisitive, fella." He glanced at the sky, where several crows were wheeling. "Inquisitive people can end up being bird-feed, understand?"

McCall nodded. Blake's not answering was as good as a yes to him, a yes with a capital "Y." The two were the men he hunted, all right, and this was the Kill 'em All gang. For one grim moment, McCall was tempted to pull his .45 out and shoot the pair dead. He would die, that was certain, but he would have accomplished his mission. His terrible anger boiled up inside like hot lava. His emotions were so intense that he trembled visibly, and one of the men riding near him noticed.

Misunderstanding, he said, "Blake won't kill you—provided you turn out right."

McCall nodded but said nothing, afraid to trust his voice. He stifled the impulse to shoot with great effort. He simply could not shoot yet. He had no certain proof these were the men who killed his wife and daughter. He had only the word of two now-dead outlaws, who could have been lying for any number of reasons. He needed proof. Blake and Scar might be killers, but he, McCall, was not. He had killed, yes, but only out of necessity, and always on the side of the law.

The only way to be sure about Blake and Scar would be to draw them out, to get them to admit what he wanted to know personally. But how to get to them? They rode ahead of the bunch, and it would be too noticeable for him to join them. The new kid on the block didn't hobnob with the leaders. He'd have to wait for the right minute.

They moved slowly, keeping well off the road now. McCall didn't know where Easton was, but the town couldn't be far, considering the pace at which they were moving. He noticed that from time to time, either Blake or Scar drifted back among the men and made small talk. It was a smart tactic. Keep in touch with the men, let 'em know you're human, and the men were with you. Stand off, stay aloof, and you let yourself in for criticism, and criticism could lead to rebelliousness. Blake and Scar were evidently smart enough to know that, so they kept in touch.

McCall realized that would have to be his opportunity, and he waited. His chance came when Scar slowed, allowing the men to jog alongside.

"Hey," Scar said jovially, "we can do pretty well on the Easton take."

"How much money you reckon?" asked Wolf.

"Heard about twenty thousand, maybe more."

Wolf nodded, satisfied.

"How about witnesses?" McCall cut in quietly. "I don't want witnesses."

"Oh, don't worry," was Scar's confident reply. "We never leave anybody around that can talk. That's why they call us the . . ." He stopped with a quick glance at Blake's back.

"The Kill 'em Alls?" McCall prompted.

"You ask too many questions," the other growled. "How come?"

"I never leave anybody myself," McCall replied in a hard voice. "I just don't want anybody left, is all. It's policy—a matter of business."

Scar stared at him. The man had pale eyes, and one had a habit of wandering off, so that McCall wasn't sure if he was looking at him, or at a rock butte over his shoulder.

"A matter of business, eh?" Scar nodded. "Yeah, well that's how we feel about it, all right."

"I've always been that way, even with the James boys, though they sometimes let witnesses live."

"That was their downfall."

"Yeah. When I was in Texas, I pulled a few jobs, but nobody ever caught me."

"How come you're up here?"

"Oh, a man likes to travel, you know. Fresh places bring new ideas for business."

"So you're a Texican?"

"Guess you could say that. Ever been there?"

It was a loaded question, and since the outlaw breed seldom spoke of past trails,

McCall wasn't sure if it would be answered. Yet, he'd been deliberately free and easy with his own past trails, hoping it would lead the way.

Scar didn't answer, so McCall added some more bait. "I pulled some big jobs down there. Maybe the biggest was around Postville."

That brought a response. The pale eyes lit up, and the wandering one held fast for a moment. "Postville? Well me and Blake was around there for a while. Yeah. Good country."

"I'd of still been there, except for the posse. That outfit was tough."

"Yeah. But we did pretty well until they broke us up."

"Feller named McCall, he was the one. I'm going back after him one of these days." McCall pointed a finger, a mock pistol. "Bang, right in the back, and that'll end him."

"McCall?" Scar scratched his head. "Him? I don't think he's around there any more, from what I heard."

"Oh?"

"Yeah. He left that country. Me and Blake made a raid on his place, almost at the last there, and we wiped him out. Oh, he got a couple of our boys after that, the Sideracks, I heard. Had 'em hung. I heard their brother, Turk, is after him, too, that's what I heard."

"You say you wiped out McCall?"

"Yeah, got—" Suddenly the pale eyes turned even more pale. "Hey, I'm talkin' too much." He forced his pony ahead, and the conversation ended.

McCall jogged along with the other men, as if no change had taken place. To them he looked the same as ever, a red-bearded man with black hair, a strange contrast. Some of the men in the gang were already calling him "the Texican Rainbow." It was a land of nicknames, a more certain identification than names, which were often false. Scar, unbeknownst to himself, was called Running Eye.

But under the calm beard, McCall struggled with himself. He had never struggled more fiercely with an outlaw in hand-to-hand combat during the Rustler's War. He had never wanted to kill somebody so much as he wanted Scar, and the man's back made a perfect target. Shooting him in the back would not, to McCall, constitute any breach of honor. The man was a killer, scum, who had probably often killed without a thought. Shooting him in the back would be too good for him. Yet there was still the final proof, the actual admission that he and Blake had pulled triggers that ended the lives of the most beloved people in his life. And he wanted that. He had to have that.

So he fought his terrible emotional battle to a standstill for the second time that morning. Somehow, he would have to find a way to make Scar talk. He withdrew into himself, afraid of his tongue, though Blake dropped back a couple of more times. Patience! He was within striking distance, and he did not want to ruin it.

It was nearly sundown, before Blake signaled a stop. In the distance lay a town. It rose out of the prairie suddenly, like a shout in the night, and ended as abruptly. A typical Plains town, dependent on cattle ranching for its existence. In the dying sunlight, McCall made out the silhouettes of false-fronted buildings.

The band dismounted, and their leaders drew them together for plans.

"How many know Easton?" Blake asked.

Most of men did. McCall shook his head.

"All right," Blake pointed. "See that tallest place?"

Light was fading quickly, but McCall made it out, and nodded. He was still caught in a red rage, and didn't dare speak, lest the sound of his own voice give him away. Any leader of any type of a group would challenge the anger in his voice.

"That's the bank," said Blake, "our target. The town is small, so all you have to do is foller us afterward to get out."

Again McCall nodded. How was he going to get those two to admit they were the ones?

"We'll split in two bunches," decided Blake. "I'll take one, Scar the other. Scar's people will keep guard—mine will break into the bank and get the money. I know exactly where it is. There should be no hitch. If anybody sees us good enough to identify us, kill him."

"Or them," added Scar with a crazy, sly grin.

"Agreed," murmured Wolf.

The others nodded, including Shooky, whom McCall took to be a little easier than the rest.

From then on it was lie low and wait. The men smoked and ate a cold meal of hardtack and jerky. They checked their weapons several times and made sure their horses were watered at a nearby stream. They spoke of previous robberies with the Kill 'em All gang, and, often, alone. They were loners, as lobo wolves were loners, outcasts of society, seeking society with their own kind from time to time. Most had been with the gang since its beginnings, and were happy with its success. They lived dangerously and had lost members to the guns of those they robbed, but if death beckoned, that was part of the risk for big gains.

McCall ate his jerky and hardtack, too, and listened to the stories whispered in the dark. It chilled him to know that these men with whom he rubbed shoulders would also rub him out in a second if they suspected treason. They appeared so ordinary! Actually, only Scar looked like a criminal. The others, including skinny Blake, would pass for run-of-the-mill cowhands. The average citizen would take them for just that. The contrast between the looks and the intentions of the men bemused McCall. He had noticed it before in the Rustler's War. Crooks were just like—people!

He waited quietly, seething inside, calm

as butter on the outside. One of the men remarked that, "Rainbow is sure a cool one."

McCall merely nodded.

The hour drew near, and he still hadn't thought of a way to get a confession out of Scar or Blake. Then, suddenly, welcome as fresh water in the desert, he had it. He knew what had to be done. The solution had been there all the time. It was highly dangerous, but very simple. He sat back and waited. It wouldn't be long now.

At a quarter to twelve, Blake asked the group if there were any questions. There were none.

"All right." Blake nodded toward the town, which blinked with a few lights. "Let's go."

They rode into town, and Blake's bunch stopped in front of the bank. Scar's group dismounted, and placed themselves discreetly in a half-ring in front of the doors. McCall had made sure he was with Scar, and he stood next to him now. He watched as the other bunch forced an entry into the bank then stuck his gun in Scar's ear.

"You," he said loudly, "killed my wife and daughter."

"What . . . ?" Scar whirled. "What's going on?"

"I'm McCall. Remember that woman and girl you and your partner killed near Postville?"

Scar jumped back. "You!" he gasped.

"Yes," McCall said, still loudly, "it's me, and I come to kill you."

"I told Blake we should've got you in Postville," hissed Scar, and he fired point-blank.

McCall felt the slug tear into him, and he fired back. He fired until his weapon was empty and Scar lay on ground. He fired, and each shot roared not only with powder, but his own grief and rage. He fired into the still body, and it jerked as the heavy .45 caliber lead plowed into him.

There was a clamor in the bank, the sound of boots running. Scar's half of the gang, confused by the turn of events, ran for their horses.

"What's going on?" cried Blake. "What's all this shooting?" When he saw the outside guards riding off frantically, he fired at them, yelling, "Come back here. Come back. Scar, what's going on?"

"I killed him," said McCall, "and now I'm killing you."

He ducked low, found Scar's weapon, and fired it at Blake, who fired back. The two exchanged shots in the dark, and McCall scored a hit. He heard Blake curse and cry, "I got it in the arm, boys. Help me up on my horse."

He did not to make it to his horse. The sheriff and four or five men came running, and the rest of the Kill 'em All gang fled, leaving their leaders. One was dead, and the other wounded, but very much alive, as the sheriff's men closed in.

"I'll get you, Pitt," screeched Blake. "I'll get you for this."

"The name's McCall," came the reply, in a terrible, thunderous voice, "and I'm killing you."

He fired but missed, and then he was charged by the sheriff's men. He fought with the savage strength of a man who has lived with grief too long. He fought with the strength of a man who has come within a hair's breadth of winning a long quest, only to lose, because he, himself, was losing. McCall's wound was taking its toll, and only sheer anger and guts enabled him to fight at all. He wanted one more shot at Blake. Just one more, but he couldn't get it. He tried with all his might to free himself from the struggling men and shoot Blake, but his strength ebbed as the shock of his wound set in. He toppled like a giant tree whose base was riddled with dry rot. He fell into the arms of those who fought him, but, as he went, he cried in his still terrible voice, "You're dead, Blake. You are dead."

And Blake, whose own wound now laid him low, heard, and he cursed the voice. It was a voice he vowed to quiet forever.

Chapter Eight

Lottie Branch stood on the porch of her house. She raised her nose slightly and sniffed, the way Indians tested the wind for signs. She smelled trouble. The October weather had been nasty, the worst she'd seen, in a lifetime of Plains Octobers. The wind scurried low over the flatlands, like an invisible scythe, carrying frost and freezing. Lottie's nose told her it wasn't over. The wind was colder than before, more ominous, and she shivered. Dark clouds on the horizon, towering over the earth like deranged gods, seemed to fall toward her. They were snow-bearing clouds,

clouds that, along with the wind, could destroy all in their path.

She shivered, both with apprehension and the cold, and was about to return to the warmth of the house when she stopped. She stopped and stared at a lone figure riding toward the ranch. The figure slouched in his saddle and clung to the pommel. He swayed back and forth, in a haphazard manner, as if he were drunk. His head was bare, revealing dark hair, but the red beard offered a strange contrast. His eyes were dark, the pupils dilated to catch the dim light, and his lips were parched dry from inner fires.

Lottie recognized the horse first, and she uttered an involuntary cry. "Dogs!"

The horse ambled over to the sound of her voice, and she grabbed the reins. The horse was not in good shape either. From the looks of him, Lottie judged he had come a long distance. His withers were concave like two buffalo wallows, and his nose was hot and dry.

"Lon!" she cried, above the rising wind. "Come help."

The bunkhouse wasn't far, and Lon emerged. He ran over, and between the two of them, they managed to get McCall down. There was a time, not long before, when Lon wouldn't have dreamed of carrying the big man by himself, but the once well-fleshed frame was wasted, thin as grass he told the boys in the bunkhouse later. He carried McCall inside easily, and Lottie directed him to a ground-level bedroom.

"Good heavens." She winced. "Look at that."

Dried blood covered the front of McCall's shirt.

"Go get the doctor in town," ordered Lottie, whereupon McCall's eyes opened slightly.

"Don't," he whispered, "don't go for the doctor. Bullet hole. He'll tell the law."

Lottie hesitated. She glanced at Lon.

"Well, ma'am," said the foreman, "we know he ain't a bad one, don't we?"

"You're right, Lon, but can we fix him?"

Lon grinned. "You forgetting who did the doctoring on roundups?"

Lottie flushed. She had been the one, and knew quite a bit about frontier medicine.

"Help me get his clothes off, then." Seeing Lon's glance, she added, "Don't worry about me. We have to see what's going on under that shirt, and"—she wrinkled her nose—"he needs a bath. You and the boys can do that."

"Yes ma'am."

The wound was high in the right side. Lottie noticed that it wasn't infected, though it had broken open and bled. The lack of infection was strange. After McCall had been stripped to the waist, Lon went for more help.

"And see to it that Dogs is taken care of," Lottie called after him. "The poor critter can barely stand."

McCall had lapsed into silence. At times his eyes closed and he seemed to sleep, but they popped open suddenly. Once he tried to sit up, crying in his jagged voice, "I'll get you, Blake." Then he broke off, mumbling, only to come back with a stentorian roar that belied his weakness. "Belle! Kathy! Belle!"

Lottie waited until the men had washed his thin body and slipped clean, long-handled underwear over it. Then she tended the wound. The bullet had gone all the way through McCall, so there were two ruptures for Lottie to apply her medicines to. She had taken care of snakebite, broken limbs, cuts, and rope burns, but never bullet holes. She decided that these were no different than any other explosion on the nature of man's skin, and did as she thought best.

For the first two days, McCall was in and out of it. At times he was a raging madman, crying out curses against Scar and Blake, swearing he would kill them if it was the last thing he ever did. At other times he cried, "I got you, Scar, and now, Blake! Blake, you killer of mothers and children! You who destroyed my life."

During these times, McCall's voice was very clear, like that of an actor delivering lines on the stage. But Lottie knew the thin, delirious man, who now depended on her for his life, was not acting. He was remembering, and what his mind slipped back to was something that had driven him to the very edge of sanity.

She had known from their previous encounter that he was a man on a quest. He had apparently run into his goal, and that goal was armed. There'd been a fight, and he had got somebody named Scar. There was still Blake. With a chill, she recalled the visit of Turk Siderack. The man was after McCall, and that man was a bad one. Where was he now? Close? Far? Would Blake be after McCall, too? And McCall had been afraid of the law. What had happened out there beyond the horizon? What had happened in the life of this man, who lay on a bed in her house, and whom she was shielding? Was she hiding a criminal? She shed the thought quickly. Lon had agreed that this was not a bad one, and Lon, working with the toughest breed of man on earth, knew men. Yet the law was after him. . . .

Lottie didn't ponder the questions too deeply. There was little use in that. She'd take her chances with the sheriff in Haystock, if he should come looking. In the meantime, she had a patient to heal.

At the end of three days, McCall came out of his delirium.

He sat up in bed late one afternoon, just as the last rays of sun were tilting shadows in the room.

"Where," he asked, "am I?"

"You're at the Running B," Lottie told him. She went to his side. "Don't you really know?"

McCall studied her. His eyes were clear, Lottie noted, not the opaque muddiness they had been even moments before.

McCall nodded slowly. "Oh, yes, I know now. I just didn't realize I'd made it." His eyes traveled around the room. "How long have I been here?"

"A week."

"And Dogs?"

"Getting fat in the barn."

McCall sighed and lay back in bed. He was alert, but very weak, and his muscles ached.

"Want some soup?" Lottie was anxious. "We couldn't get much down you—you kept fighting somebody called Blake."

"Did I talk about him?" McCall's voice was growing stronger. "What did I say?"

"I take it you don't like him."

"Yes."

"That," the girl's voice was soft, "you want to—kill him, McCall."

"Then he's still alive . . ."

It was a mysterious statement, but soon to be cleared up.

"I couldn't remember if I got him during the break. I guess not."

He was fading, weakness stealing his power like a subtle drug, and he fell asleep. When he awoke, the faded early November sun was struggling to throw beams on his blankets. The room was empty, and he lay quietly, trying to put his mind together. He was at the Running B, and he was in the care of Lottie Branch. As his mind dug into the situation, he remembered that the Running B had been his goal ever since escaping from Easton jail. He'd made it! God knows how many miles he and Dogs traveled to get here, but here he was. The big question: Why had he chosen the Running B? He was putting good people in jeopardy.

Lottie entered, smiling. "About time," she greeted him. "You were out for nearly twenty-four hours. Now," she urged, "how about that soup?"

McCall was suddenly ravenous. Weeks of undernourishment, weeks of nursing a painful wound, had taken his appetite and thrown it to the prairie dogs. But now that he was on the mend, he could feel it, and by heaven, he was starved.

"Miss Branch," he said, "I appreciate your offer of soup—but I'd just as soon get wrapped around steak and potatoes."

"You," she responded with a smile that cast rays much stronger than the sun, "are on the mend. Steak it is."

While she was gone, McCall again pondered the question: Why had he chosen the Running B for refuge? He was a stranger here, and yet, even as he lay on a prison cot, he thought of the Running B. He felt, for reasons unexplained, that he would be welcomed.

When Lottie returned with a steak the size of a serving platter, along with pan-fried potatoes, canned peas, and a piece of pie large enough to feed a family, she said, "I have a question for you. You don't have to answer."

"I owe you," mumbled McCall, injecting a great bite of steak into a welcoming mouth.

"Why did you come here?"

McCall shook his head. "I don't know. It's a mystery to me, and yet, I didn't feel there was any place else to go." He looked at the girl. "I'm wanted by the law."

"I know."

"You should turn me in. You could get in trouble."

"Yes, I should. Do you want to tell me what it's all about?"

McCall nodded. "Yes, I owe you that, too."

He told her first about why he was on the road at all, about his wife and daughter. He told her about his suspicions and his quest to get the murderers, Blake and Scar.

The girl reacted with horror. "How can men be so awful?"

McCall shook his head, his face sad, remembering again the crumpled bodies of his wife and daughter. "I don't know. The Rustler's War was one thing, man against man, but killing women and children?" He swore violently. "I don't know!"

Lottie ignored the language. She'd heard it all before, and it made no impression as such. What touched her was the deep grief of the man who lay before her.

She was curious. "The Rustler's War?"

McCall told her about his part in it, how he had helped end the terror of the time. "I was," he added, "a lawman, then. Now"— he smiled wryly—"I'm outside the law for finishing a job that was once legal."

"Confusing."

"Yes."

There was quiet, except for the business of diminishing McCall's ravenous appetite. Then Lottie broke the silence with, "How did you get wounded, and why are you on the outside of the law?"

Without hesitation, as if he were confiding in a friend he'd known for years instead of a scant few days, McCall told Lottie about his joining the Kill 'em All gang, hoping to catch up to Blake and Scar. He told of his partial success, getting Scar, but of his failure to get Blake after being wounded.

"Just couldn't get Blake," he said quietly, "but I aim to. Oh yes, I aim to."

"You were caught with him and thrown into jail, as a member of the Kill 'em All gang?"

"That's it. I did put a slug in Blake, though, and I got one from Scar, so the town doctor treated us."

"That explains why your wound wasn't more infected than it was."

"I suppose."

"How did you escape?"

"Blake's men came for him a week later. They rode up to the jail, held the sheriff and his men on the business end of .45s, and got him out. Blake took me as well." McCall laughed, a dry, rasping sound, like wind on winter wheat. "I knew why Blake wanted to spring me. I'd killed his partner, foiled a burglary, and landed him in prison. He could have had me shot right there, but for what I'd done, he wanted leisure. He wanted to send me to hell on a slow train."

Lottie shuddered. "Torture?"

McCall nodded, then went on.

"But I ran for it. It was night—those birds work best at night, except for one thing, they can't see very far. I ran for a building that looked like a stable, found Dogs, and we hit the open prairie."

"Still, I'd have thought Blake would have followed you."

"They started to do just that, but Blake made one mistake. He didn't kill the sheriff and his men—very unlike Blake's usual style. The law got into the act then, firing at anything that moved, so Blake and his bunch had to get out of town."

"And now you are here."

"Yes."

McCall was finishing his meal, wiping up the last of his steak juice with a biscuit. Again silence fell over the room. McCall had told his story. There was nothing left to say, but the silence was not as easy as before. An unspoken question lingered with so much presence as to be tangible, like the pressure of a damp fog.

Lottie voiced the question. "What," she asked, "is next?"

McCall, having already encountered the question in his mind, had the answer ready.

"When I was in jail, I told the sheriff

why I was after Blake and Scar. I told him of my part in the Rustler's War, and that before they tried me, I'd like him to get in touch with Postville authorities. I thought that my part in that business might get me off, or a lesser sentence. I never found out because Blake's men came along."

"Wouldn't it have been a good idea to go back to the sheriff, when there was a chance?"

"I thought of it, but the sheriff would have kept me in jail until he found out about me, and I was a sitting duck for Blake if I was behind bars. I haven't any doubt he already has his spies looking."

"Don't you think he's forgotten about you?"

"No. He's looking. He'll look till he finds me, I hope."

"And the law?"

"I'm going into Haystock as soon as I can to get the law off my back. I'm sure that by now word is all over this country about me."

"You don't have only Blake and the law to worry about."

"Oh?"

"Ever hear of a man named Turk Siderack?"

McCall remembered his conversation with the member of the Kill 'em Alls. He nodded. "Yeah, something. Those two brothers of his"—McCall almost spit, he was so disgusted—"they deserved more than hanging. Rotten filth!"

"This man, Turk, is dangerous."

"Good." McCall was savage. "That's the way I like 'em." He was curious. "How did you know about him?"

Lottie explained Siderack's visit.

McCall shrugged. "If he feels that way, that's the way he feels. I'll be happy to meet him."

"He was a terrible person—spoke too softly, looked like a bulldog. He made me shiver. Be careful. A back shot would mean nothing to him."

McCall found he was pleased with Lottie's concern, but he said, "I've been dealing with a lot of people who fight that way. It doesn't worry me."

"Why did you come back to the Running B?"

The question took McCall off guard for a moment, and he found himself flustered.

He finally mustered an answer. "I don't rightly know, to tell the truth." He paused, then added, "Yes, I guess I know. I didn't dare hit but only a town or two for supplies. I didn't want to get tangled with the law. I needed someplace to go for this"—he pointed to his healing wound—"and, well, just to be here, I guess."

"And you thought I'd take you in?"

"I'm sorry, if I'm wrong."

Lottie smiled. "You were right—though, like you, I don't 'rightly know' why. You are an outlaw, after all."

"That's something I have to get straightened out."

Lottie was alarmed. Her eyes clouded.

"I'd advise against going to Haystock," she said quickly.

"Why?"

"Well, the law might not be so lenient as you hope. How do you know they have word from Postville yet?"

"Would it matter if I became a jailbird?"

It was the girl's turn to fend off confusion. "Well," she said, "I don't like to think of anybody locked up. You know?"

"I like you, Miss Branch. Is that all right?"

Lottie nodded quickly, shy. "Yes, Mr. McCall, it's all right."

McCall grinned. "Then we have that settled."

"What's that?"

"We like each other."

The girl was amused. "I think you could say that."

"All right. Then with that out of the way, I have to clear myself in Haystock."

"I wish you wouldn't."

"No, you don't wish that. You don't want me caught, but you want me cleared, Lottie, and in order to clear myself I have to face—who's the sheriff?"

"Tucker."

"The sooner the better."

The girl nodded. "Yes."

"I'll go today."

"Isn't that a little soon? You aren't well yet."

"Well enough."

Lottie could see the man with the red beard and black hair was determined.

"Do you want Lon to go along with you?"

"Why?"

"Well—in case there's trouble with— you know, Blake or Turk—he could help."

McCall reached for the girl's hand and clasped it in his own. "You think that much of me, you'd risk your own men?"

"Looks like it."

McCall kissed her and the girl drew close. "Oh, McCall," she whispered, "what a dreadful business."

"I don't think it's so dreadful."

"Why? You might be killed."

"Yes, but it brought me back here, and to you."

Lottie nodded, and McCall kissed her again. "Did you ever think it was possible for two people to meet who were exactly right for each other?"

"No."

"Well, it happened."

"Yes. Yes, my dear, it surely did."

"Now, then, Lon or one of the boys can saddle Dogs for me, if they will."

"Yes."

She drew as close as she could to this man, this near stranger who had brought love into her life, and she marveled. It happened so suddenly—or had it? She'd found herself thinking of McCall in the months he was gone, thinking about him quite a bit. Had those thoughts been signals of an love? Could have been. Could very well have been.

"I'll get my gun."

"Maybe it would be best to go without it."

"In one sense, yes, the sheriff would appreciate that. So would Blake and Turk."

"Better wear it."

"Could you see to my horse." McCall flexed his arms. "I've got more meat on me than a week ago, but I'm still weak."

The girl left and McCall made sure his weapon was ready. Then he mounted Dogs and left. The girl watched after him. "Be careful," she whispered to herself, "be careful, my man. I want you in my life."

McCall was weaker than he thought, and the first mile was difficult. He kept getting dizzy spells, and his wound ached, but after a mile, with his blood pumping, he rode easily enough and had time to put his mind to matters other than his health. He thought of Lottie. She'd looked forlorn as he left—forlorn, but not helpless. There was nothing helpless about Lottie Branch, and yet there was the woman in her, who wanted everything safe and regular. There was also the beauty in her that radiated like an inner sun that new love brought. Lottie! If anybody in the world, and he'd told himself this before, could take his wife's place, it would be Lottie. McCall was not a praying man, but he thanked God now. Every now and then, he thanked God for something, and this was one of those times. It was definitely one of those times.

He turned his mind to what lay ahead. Sheriff Tucker—what kind of man was he? How would their meeting go? And if he was forced to use his gun, would he? McCall could make no decision about that. He would have to wait and see. But no matter what happened, he could not return to the Running B, not to Lottie. He couldn't bring the law back to her.

"What'll we meet, Dogs my friend. Eh?" And the horse waggled his ears.

Far to the west, across the Wolf Mountains, were two men. One was the head of a gang of killers, the other a lone wolf. The two met because the lone wolf wanted that. They met, and the loner joined the gang.

"We have," he told Turk, "a stage to rob, and witnesses to send to heaven."

The other laughed coarsely. They were two of a kind. Turk Siderack worked alone, but Blake could be useful in tracking McCall. It would be beneficial to forfeit a little independence for the greater gain. Further, an occasional alliance with a gang didn't hurt. One learned new tricks. Though vicious himself in dealing with his victims, Turk had not always killed them, nor had he been particularly wary of witnesses. He found he liked Blake's policy of killing them all. It left no loose ends, and any man in their profession would agree that was good business.

Chapter Nine

McCall guided Dogs toward Haystock with confidence. It had been over a month since he escaped from the Easton jail. By now, word should have reached the lawmen in this part of the country that he was not an outlaw, that he had, in fact, been instrumental in the Rustler's War. Quite instrumental, if he did say so. The fact was, he had almost single-handedly led the ranchers in their fight. What was more, he had been sworn in as a deputy marshal. He couldn't be much more on the side of the law than that.

Haystock was not a large town, but it fit the needs of the area. It was a supply depot, in essence, a place where cattlemen bought what they needed. The railroad was a hundred miles north, and Haystock also centered as a buyer's meeting place for the region. Much money changed hands, and Haystock was solvent.

The lone main street seemed to welcome him, as McCall entered. There was the usual buzz from the bars, the storekeepers sweeping dirt and dust from the boardwalks, the loafers tilted back in chairs under porch awnings. It was a peaceful scene, a usual scene, one that made McCall feel at home. Postville was much like this.

He stopped Dogs in front the sheriff's office and dismounted. He hitched the horse to the rail and entered the building. There were three men inside. Two of them were shuffling papers, and one, a short man with steely eyes, sat in a wooden swivel chair, his thumbs hooked in his black woollen vest. All were armed with pistols.

"I'm looking for the sheriff," McCall said. He had a hunch the short man was him, according to Lottie's description.

"I'm Tucker," said the man, "the one you're looking for. What can I do for you?"

The voice was tough, a hard voice, a voice that dealt with criminals on a daily

basis and had lost its capacity for pleasant-
ries.

"My name is McCall, and I've come to
get something straightened out."

Sheriff Tucker was on his feet, moving,
despite his stocky body, with the smooth-
ness of cat. His pistol was out.

"Why, Mr. McCall," he said with a grin,
"how nice of you to walk right in."

McCall was startled. He felt a tug of apprehension, like undertow in a seemingly
calm river.

"Sheriff, why the gun?"

"You know why, bucko." Tucker raised
his voice. "Hey, boys, looky who just gave
us a present."

The deputies were already on their way.
They grinned, even as their boss grinned,
and one said, "Well, I'll be a steer's
mother, if this isn't a new one on me."

"Relieve him of his hardware," ordered
Tucker, and McCall's gun was hoisted
from its holster.

"I don't understand," objected McCall.
"Haven't you got word from Postville yet?"

"About what, feller?" The sheriff nodded
at the deputies. "Lock this flying outlaw
up."

McCall backed off. "You arresting me for that bank thing in Easton?"

"You are certainly smart, son."

"But I wasn't a member of the gang. I told the sheriff there to get in touch with Postville—I'd be cleared."

"Oh?"

"I was a leader in the Rustler's War. I was a deputy, and was after Blake and Scar—they headed the Kill 'em All gang."

"You a deputy now?"

"The posse was disbanded."

"Then you got no right killing a man, even somebody like Scar. That's the law's job."

"The sheriff in Postville will clear me, I tell you." McCall was beginning to feel the emptiness of defeat. Something had gone wrong.

"Well, he ain't so far. Right now, all I know is you're a thug in the Kill 'em Alls, my friend." The hard voice was brittle. "We got word about that, and I want you people. Oh, yes. We'll use you as bait—let it be known you are here. Grand, eh? Your boys will come to get you, just like at Easton, only we'll be ready."

"They'll come to kill me," said McCall bitterly.

"Now, now, no tantrums. You had your fun killing all those innocent people, and now we'll have ours. The judge is due in two weeks. We'll have a very quick trial and then hang you." The sheriff made a jerking motion with his fist. "You'll go to that great robbers' roost in the sky." He grinned. "We have good justice here."

McCall was shoved, none too gently, into a cell. His wound throbbed, and he was angry with himself for being so stupid. If the Easton sheriff had sent a wire to Postville, there wasn't time for word to get to Haystock. There was no telegraph in Haystock as yet. A telegraph network might have saved him.

He sat on the dirty bunk and thought about his situation. He was in a tight spot. As far as Tucker was concerned, he had an outlaw in custody. A circuit judge was coming in two weeks. They didn't fool with outlaws. They were given hefty sentences or hanged, depending on the mood of the country and the judge. As a supposed member of Blake's gang, McCall didn't fool himself: A rope waited for him.

How could he get out of it? Would word come from the Postville sheriff, and if it did, would that word make any difference?

McCall grunted and stretched mightily, easing tensed nerves.

There was an alternative, and that was breaking out. He was surely not prepared to sit in a cell like a chicken waiting for the roasting pan. Better to be a free quasi-outlaw than a dead wimp. McCall made his decision: He would break out at the first chance. Even if he was killed in the attempt, it would be worth the gamble. Once out, he'd head for Postville himself and get sworn statements as to who he was.

The day passed in silence. There were no other prisoners in jail, and the place was eerie, like the inside of a catacomb. Window-bar shadows, thrown on the floor by the cool sun, were straight and sterile, offering no relief from the relentless claustrophobic effect.

His jailers, with little to do themselves, visited now and then with questions.

"How could you kill people in cold blood?" Tucker wanted to know. "I've had to down a few, but it was always them or me."

"I didn't kill anybody defenseless, ever," McCall declared.

"What's that bunch like?" asked a deputy. "Do they drink blood like I hear?"

"At least that pig, Scar, is gone," said Tucker. "They say you killed him."

"That's right. I did."

"Didn't want to split the take, right? Got mad and shot him?"

"No—he killed my wife and daughter, him and Blake, like I said. I want Blake, too," and McCall added the last with such savagery and hate that Tucker looked at him quizzically.

"You know," he said, "I almost believe you. Almost." He grinned. "But a dog could tell a better story than that. You'll hang, McCall, or whatever your name is. You'll hang."

That afternoon, Lottie came. She was pale, and her eyes were dark with concern.

The sheriff was curious. "How come you know this murderous rat, Lottie?"

"He's not a murderous rat, Sheriff Tucker," was the crisp reply. "He's a good man. I will vouch for that."

"Well, he's a member of the Kill 'em Alls, and if that's good, I'm a donkey's cousin."

Lottie didn't respond to the remark. She knew there was little sense in wasting time trying to convince the sheriff that McCall wasn't what he seemed. The sheriff had to go by facts—and the facts told him McCall was an outlaw.

"May I see him?" she asked.

"Of course, though why"—the sheriff was still mystified—"you want to is beyond me."

The cells were in a back room, and the sheriff left her with his prisoner.

"I told you it would be dangerous to come to Haystock," she said to McCall angrily.

"Had to do it, Lottie. I have to clear my name."

"Well, this isn't doing it, exactly."

"No, but what would you want—hide out at your place and put you cahoots with a criminal?"

"You're no criminal!"

"The law thinks so, Lottie, and I can understand that. After all, if they believed every crook who says he's innocent, we wouldn't need lockups."

The two ceased their back-and-forth, as if they'd come to a dead end. Such wasn't the case. Lottie was thinking.

"I'll smuggle you a gun," she whispered fiercely. "You can break out."

McCall stared. "You'd do that for me?"

"Of course."

"Of course? Why 'of course'?"

"I think you are innocent."

"Do you love me that much, Lottie, as to put yourself outside the law?"

The girl nodded without hesitation.

They were speaking through the cell bars.

"Step closer," McCall requested.

Lottie did, and they kissed, and in her kiss McCall felt the passion that told him this woman, this fine person, would risk her reputation—in a country where reputations counted—to save the man she loved.

"I'll have no guns smuggled," McCall said quietly, but with great joy in his heart. "I won't let you do that Lottie. Now, I'll tell you what it is we will do."

"Tell me, then." The girl was watching him with shining eyes.

"We'll wait. Word will come, I'm sure of it. We'll just have to wait—go by the law, Lottie. I learned that in the Rustler's War. The law is sometimes slow, but it is the right way to go."

"That's final?"

"Yes. Now you go home and don't worry, but," McCall added, "don't forget me, either."

"Do you think I could? I'll be here every

day. Every day, my dear, dumb, honest, McCall."

"Still angry?"

"Yes." The girl laughed. "I'm angry at your coming in, and so happy that I'm here. Crazy, eh?"

"Yep. Crazy."

Lottie kissed him, and couldn't resist, "The quality of love is strained." She pointed at the bars.

"I think you are feeling better," was the dry, amused response.

When Lottie reached the outer sheriff's office, Tucker stopped her with, "How long you been hiding him?"

"I haven't . . ."

"Don't lie to me, girl. Think I don't know the signs when I see them?"

There was a window in the door to the cell block. Lottie knew at once what had happened.

"You've been spying!" she accused, enraged.

"Of course. It's my job. I saw it all, Lottie, and I don't need to tell you that two people didn't get as close as you without some preliminary contact. He went to your place after he escaped from the Easton jail, right?"

"Of course. He knew I'd take him in. And," the girl added with heat, "I'll deny I ever told you that, Sheriff Tucker, if I'm asked."

"Your denial would pack weight." The lawman nodded. "The Running B, under your father"—the words were pointed— "had a reputation for honesty. Like father, like daughter, is the way it goes here, so I won't try to press charges. But Lottie, I'm going to watch you and your men, like a hawk."

"We won't try anything, Sheriff, and that's a promise."

"Just the same, I'll watch. Love is a powerful mover and breaker of promises. I know. I was there myself."

"You?"

Lottie was, for the moment, taken out of herself. She'd known Tucker for as long as she could remember. He'd been sheriff forever, and a good one, but she'd never thought of him as having had a personal life. Could it be that this man, who had the reputation of being one of the sharpest lawmen in the country, a man entirely dedicated to his job—so much so that he seemed naked without his star—could it be he once knew about love? Lottie suddenly realized that she actually knew very little about Sheriff Tucker.

Embarrassed by this show of intimacy and her own assumptions, Lottie could only stare.

The sheriff smiled. "Oh, yes, my girl, I was in love, and I know that it can be dangerous. Don't do anything foolish, girl."

"I won't," Lottie replied, still bemused by her discovery. "We won't," she added hastily, and then she left. She rode home full of what had happened—a confirmed love for McCall in no uncertain terms, a sudden insight into a man she'd taken for granted all her life, and in her heart, riding alongside her love for McCall, a great uncertainty for him, like the sun and the rain pushing for dominance in her thoughts. What could she do? The sheriff would keep his word, and both she and her men would be watched. The girl's thoughts were confusing. She was anxious and extremely happy at the same time, and, as a consequence, a very frustrated young woman.

In his cell, McCall was undergoing somewhat the same confusion, an ocean tide with no beach to conquer. He was not surprised to see Tucker push open the door.

His eyes were as bright and uncompromising as rivets on a pair of Levis.

"You scum," he said without preamble. "You sweep an innocent girl like that off her feet to get your own way. Figured she could bring a gun, eh? Or maybe her boys would break you out?"

The sheriff was so disgusted he spit on the floor.

"I think," he said in a flat voice, on which dislike rode bareback, "you are the worst." The rivet eyes narrowed. "You say you weren't really in the Kill 'em Alls? Then why were you with 'em? You say you were a top gun on the law's side in the Rustler's War? Then why hasn't the sheriff notified us?"

"It's a long way off," replied McCall, knowing his argument carried little conviction. "Word takes a long time getting here. You have no telegraph."

"Let me tell you something, mister." The sheriff stopped, and cocked an ear as if listening. "This town—I hear talk, see? A lot of people got hurt by the Kills, as they call your rotten bunch, and they know you are here. They might not want to wait for a judge to come by and say they can hang you. Judge won't be here for a while, anyway, and these people, salt of the earth they are, might want justice a little quicker."

"You are supposed to stop that."

"How can I if I'm chasing some horse thief twenty miles away?"

"So." The prisoner nodded slowly. "It is like that."

The sheriff speared him with eyes like knives. "No, you got it wrong. I won't be absent on purpose. It could just happen. I cover a big territory, not just Haystock."

"You got two deputies."

"Sure, and one will always be here, but I'm not so certain either could hold off a mob."

"But you could?"

"Yes."

The answer was direct, and McCall knew the sheriff meant it. What was more, he felt the stocky man with the badge could, indeed, stop a mob. He could probably stop a speeding bullet with one hand. He was that kind.

The conversation ended, leaving McCall plenty to think about. He was a regular dictionary of thought, and after all thinking had been done, he came to only one conclusion: He had to escape. The only way to prove his innocence was by getting word from Postville. The quickest way was to head for Abilene, where there was a telegraph. He'd wire the Postville sheriff, get an answer, and return to Haystock. He had to prove he was who he said he was.

The big question was how to get out. The place was guarded constantly. There had to be a way, though, and McCall put his mind to it. Finally, he arrived at step one. It wasn't a step to his liking, because it involved Lottie, but there was no choice. She was his only contact.

She visited that evening, and he came right to the point.

"If I don't get out of here, vigilantes—a mob, I'd call them—will come after me."

Lottie was alarmed. "What makes you say that?"

"Tucker."

The girl understood at once. "So, he gave a warning?"

"Yes."

"I haven't known him to do that. He must think you are innocent."

"Maybe, but he'd shoot me dead if I tried to escape and he caught me at it. I'm going to have to wait, Lottie, and take my chances. Here's what I'd like you to do, and you don't have to if you don't wish it. I'll understand."

"Come on, McCall," she prompted with some irritation. "Do you think I'd be here at all if I didn't want to help? What do you want? You want a gun? I'll get it to you somehow. A horse . . . ?"

McCall raised his hand. "That's it. Find out where Dogs is and let me know."

"That's all?"

"That's enough. I want him. If I take a horse that doesn't belong to me—well." He grimaced. "You know they hang horse thieves."

Lottie wasted no time. She left and was back in half an hour.

"Dogs is in McClusky's Stables right down at the end of the street."

"And my saddle?"

"I don't know what your saddle looks like." Once again, Lottie expressed slight irritation. "You should tell me these things."

"I figured you be that smart."

"Well, I'm not!"

The air was hot for a moment, as personalities clashed. Then McCall grinned at about the same time Lottie's lips spread in a smile.

"Our first quarrel," quipped McCall. "Is this how it will be?"

The girl was at the bars in an instant, her arms reaching through, grasping McCall by the shoulders, drawing him forward.

"Oh, my dear," she murmured, "please be careful. It's nerves that are upsetting us, is all. Nerves. Your life is in danger, and I'm upset." She kissed him. "I love you, outlaw, I love you, and I want to have you safe."

"I know." McCall returned her kiss. "Don't worry. I'm a tough geezer. I'm not worried. You better go now. This setting," he glanced at the cold cells, "isn't exactly a good place to talk. Go, and thank you for what you did."

That night, when shadows loomed in the jail, McCall heard street sounds. They were peculiar, like the ebb and flow of a tide. At times they reached him, a full cacophony of human voices, all mingled and unintelligible. Then they receded to a murmur, only to rise again.

There was something ominous in that, like lightning hidden in storm clouds, a danger sensed rather than seen. As the night wore on, and the town's bars were on full duty, the din from the street grew more insistent, more intense. McCall had heard it before, during the Rustler's War, and he went back in memory to discover its significance. Suddenly he remembered, and what he recalled wasn't good: The town was going through the prelude to a hanging.

His suspicions were confirmed when some men dared come close to the jail and speak their minds.

"I tell yuh, we ought ter git him. Be a lesson to them Kill fellers—keep out of our town."

"Let's git a rope."

"Hold on. Tucker would shoot us dead, if we tried a lynching."

"He couldn't do nothin' if they's enough of us."

"You a fool? That man stood up to the Dalton boys and worked with Wyatt Earp in Dodge City. I ain't goin' against him!"

"Judge is comin' next week."

"Lynchin' is better. Shows the Kills we mean business."

There was assent to this. Then a calm voice oiled the night air. "We got a week before the judge gets here. Let's plan this out, and when Tucker is gone, we hit."

"What about his deputies?"

This seemed to be a joke. "Those two apes don't know nothin' without the sheriff tells 'em."

There was a snicker.

After that, the words faded, and McCall felt weird. He had just heard his fate decided by bodyless voices in the dark. A lynching would serve the community best, seemed to be the idea. Zealots for the public good! McCall didn't like that at all, and he allowed a disdainful burp. Good grief!

The night passed slowly for the wakeful prisoner. He planned and replanned his escape. It could be done when meals were served. Grab the guard's gun. He could do it by pretending to be sick. They'd bring a doctor in, and he could grab the guard's gun then, too. Or he could escape by simply bolting out the door at some chance moment when his cell was open.

There were a number of ways, and McCall pondered them very carefully. But when the opportunity actually came, he hadn't expected it at all. None of his plans matched.

On Saturday night, two days after his arrest, several drunks were thrown in the cell next to his. Their weapons had been taken, except for one man, who had a derringer.

"They ain't s' smarth," he bragged, with a liquored up tongue so thick it could have served as a cork in the bottle that created it. He flashed the little weapon, hidden in a hip pocket. "I ought ter shoot m' way out 'er here," he grumbled. "I'm from Texas. They can't do this t' a Texican."

McCall's ears perked up at that. "I'm from Texas, too, brother," he said. "And I agree—they can't lock up a Texican."

"No," said third man wryly, "but they done done it."

"Ain't no use t' shooting out," advised a third. "They only gonna keep us fer th' night."

"Yeah," was the general agreement. But the man from Texas eyed McCall. "What part you from?"

"Way south—south of Amarillo."

"Shore miss that country. A feller can get a little drunk, an' they don't bother him there."

"True freedom."

"Yeah."

The Texican lay down on the bunk next to McCall's cell. "Lay next to your cell," he muttered, "like being among kin."

All the men were soon snoring. As one said, they'd be let loose in the morning anyway, so sleeping it off made the time go faster.

McCall did not sleep. He had never been more awake. The indignant Texan was lying on his stomach, and his derringer bulged in a hip pocket. That little pistol was the key to freedom.

When he was certain the Texan was out of this world, he reached through the bars and, with a little difficulty, extracted the weapon. He retreated to a far corner in his cell and examined the gun. It was a double-barreled pistol, .32 caliber. They were considered nuisance guns, carried mostly by gamblers and others who lived on the edge, but despite their lightweight reputation, they were deadly. A .32 caliber slug could make a man quite dead.

McCall listened then. He heard movement in the outer office. He listened for some time but heard no voices. That was important information. Whoever was in the office was alone.

"Oh," he groaned loudly. "Ohhhh, I hurt."

The office door opened, and a guard stalked in. He thumped in his leather-soled boots to McCall's cell.

"What's the matter. Why n't you shut up?"

"I got a bellyache," complained McCall. "I need a doctor."

"Ha! Big chance you have. Our doc's got bullet holes and knife cuts to take care of tonight. He ain't gonna look after no bellyache."

"Yeah, but this one's different. You can see it."

The guard was intrigued. "See it? What you mean?"

"You have to get closer. This light's too dim to see it from far off."

"I ain't never heard of a stomachache you could see," snickered the guard, but as McCall hoped, he drew closer to the cell.

When he was up close, McCall stuck the .32 derringer in the man's belly.

"You move," he whispered, "and you are a dead man."

The guard stared down at the little pistol, horrified.

"You tricked me," he almost bleated. "You done tricked me."

"Now give me your pistol."

The guard hesitated, and McCall pressed the derringer deep into the man's somewhat portly stomach. The lawman's gun found its way into McCall's hand.

"Now open the cell—and be very quiet. Remember, I'm a member of the Kill 'em Alls, and I'd love to shoot you."

The guard was a middle-aged man with a big nose, and a liking for the things in life he could smell with it. He didn't want to be dead, and he didn't doubt the prisoner for a minute. He reached for a ring of keys hanging from his belt by a snap, and unlocked the cell.

McCall locked him in after relieving the man of his gun belt and holster.

"You start yelling before I count to ten, and I'll come back and not only shoot you, but those men in there," McCall pointed to the drunk tank.

"You'll never git far," hissed the guard. "Tucker, he'll foller you to the end of the earth."

"Good. Now shut up."

McCall left the jail swiftly, before Tucker or the other guard returned. He headed for the stable that Lottie had told him about, and found Dogs. He threw his saddle over the horse's broad back, cinched up, and tossed on his saddlebags. The bags were heavy, much heavier than when he last hefted them, but he had no time for examination. He rode out of town in the darkness very quickly. He rode toward Abilene, where there would be a telegraph. Before he reached the edge of town, he heard an explosion of cries behind him, and knew his escape had been discovered. He reached over and patted Dogs' neck.

"Hope you are rested, friend. We have a ways to go."

The horse snorted, as if he understood, and stretched out his four legs in a mighty gallop.

There was no moon, but Dogs could see the road well enough to keep on track. Curious about the bags, McCall unstrapped them and examined the contents as he bumped along. There was a pistol in one, with holster and extra ammunition. There was food—pemmican and dried beans and coffee. There was extra clothing, including underwear.

In spite of his predicament—he had no doubt that if Tucker caught up, he'd shoot first and ask questions later—McCall laughed out loud. He had no doubt, either, who'd left the stocked saddlebags. It had to

be Lottie. And she thought of extra underwear?

McCall laughed again and felt better for
it. It had been a long time since he'd had
a good laugh.

Lottie Branch. What a woman!

Chapter Ten

Turk Siderack had no trouble ingratiating himself with the Kill 'em Alls. He was a man, who played both sides of the fence. He knew the world of the lawful, the good folks who paid marshals and sheriffs to keep their lives free of crime. When at rest from criminal activities, he mingled with these folks, for they didn't suspect him. He had dinner at their tables, attended their dances, and squired their daughters.

On the other side of the fence, however, Turk Siderack knew those of the Owl Hoot Trail—the robbers, highwaymen, and killers, small-time and big-time. He was known among them as well, and very much respected. Turk Siderack had never been taken by the law. The law didn't even know what he looked like, didn't know his name. All the law knew was some hideous crimes had been committed by "person or persons unknown."

Turk had gone to Cheyenne first. It was a move based on experience. He had heard of the gang breaking their leader out of jail, a man named Blake. He knew they would not return to Leadville, or any other center in the region. Every lawman around would be looking for them. There was now a bounty of one thousand dollars on Blake's head, and five hundred each for bona fide members of the gang. The gang would move a long way off, and Cheyenne was just such a place. They would, if they played the game right, filter into town one at a time, keep a low profile, and act like honest men for a while. But they would meet, and they would plan for the day when it was right to strike again.

When he reached Cheyenne, Turk began his inquiries. He was very cautious, dropping the Kills into conversation with the toughest men he met up with. Those with hard faces and steely eyes met his approval. Those who watched the doors warily, whether shopping for beans or having one at a bar, were his special targets. Turk knew the kind very well. He was one of them.

One day, a shifty little man who called himself Shooky, seemed extra talkative.

"Seems I heard of you," the man said. "Wasn't you down in Texas for a while?"

"Could have been." Turk waited. Such personal questions were not asked unless there was a reason.

"Well," Shooky went on, "let's say you were. There's talk that you might be Turk Siderack."

Turk saw his opportunity. Shooky had made his bold statement—accusation, in a sense—and now it was time to respond.

"I want to meet Blake," he said.

"Blake?"

"Don't play dumb. I know what you're doing, and yes, I'd like to join the Kill 'em Alls."

"I didn't say anything about the Kills!" was the protest.

"Mister, you just told me all I need to know—you are a scout for them. Tell Blake I'll meet him here at sundown."

"You got me wrong, mister."

"Beat it, errand boy. Do as you're told."

Shooky flushed. He didn't like being called "errand boy" at all, but in sizing up the man who dropped the insult, he decided it was best not to take up the challenge. He had more important things to do, and he headed straight for Blake.

Blake was holed up in a hotel. Wolf was with him, but he was the only one. It had been agreed the gang would meet no more than two at a time, to discourage attention.

"You say this man is Turk Siderack?" Blake was intrigued. Usually his recruits were not such big-timers.

"He didn't tell me his name, but I recognized the mustaches. He's the only one in the West got 'em like that."

"Remember the last man you recruited, Shooky?" This was from Wolf, whose eyes narrowed on the Kill 'em Alls scout.

"Hey," protested Shooky. "You all agreed to take him. It wasn't just my fault, you know. You don't have to take Siderack, but I think you should look. Don't cost nothin' t' look, and we need another man, since we lost . . . "

Shooky stopped himself before he mentioned McCall's name. It wasn't safe to mention his last effort at all.

"McCall," hissed Blake.

Shooky nodded unhappily.

Blake's scrawny frame seemed to harden into a steel lance. His eyes blazed with deep fury. "McCall," he repeated, "the man who nearly broke us up. We got to get him. Got to!" He banged his fist on a table with such force that a glass lampshade leaped out of its socket and broke on the floor.

"I want McCall," Blake hissed again, a thousand furies sharpening his voice to a spearhead. "I want him! There's a thousand on my head—well, I've offered two thousand to the man who brings me *his* head, dead or alive." He laughed nastily at his joke. "Two thousand!"

"Then, should I tell Siderack?" Shooky wanted to know. He was hoping for a yes, because he didn't want to disappoint his new find either. It seemed to him that the man with the mustaches would not take refusal very well.

Blake nodded. "We'll meet at the Dawn Tavern."

"That's where he'll be," said Shooky happily. It was working out well.

Blake had no trouble picking out his man. The mustache was enough. He sidled up to him at the bar.

"I understand," he said conversationally, "that you are looking for a job."

Turk eyed the other savagely, "Now who gave you that notion . . ." His voice trailed off, and he took in the speaker with interest. "A job? Depends."

"They tell me you are Turk Siderack."

"Who are *they?*"

"Word gets around. After all, it pays to know who the competition is."

"Good business," Turk agreed. "What are you offering?"

"Shall we go to my room? More privacy."

Wolf was there, and Turk was immediately suspicious.

"He's my most trusted man," Blake said. "What we say, I want him to hear. If I'm killed, he takes over."

Turk couldn't disagree with that. After all, it wasn't his gang, and he realized there had to be an understood succession, in case something went wrong.

He said, "I want a straight answer to this question—I can't waste time with amateurs. You are the Kill 'em Alls?"

Blake glanced at Wolf, and the two were silent for a moment. They'd been very nearly broken up by the last recruit, and were cautious.

"Unless you have a good reason for not telling me, I am not interested," said Turk. "Listen," he pressed, "you know me, or think you do. You know I work alone usually, but I have a reason for wanting to join you. I want to be backed by the best for this job."

"Job?"

Blake was more than curious. Was this man going to tell him what jobs were in line? Nobody told Blake what to do.

"Yes, I'm after a man named McCall. Ever hear of him?"

Blake nearly exploded. "Hear of him? Mister, he's mine! I want to skin him alive—and I mean that." He stopped, and looked at Turk shrewdly. "Has he done you dirt, too?"

"He had my brothers hanged during the Rustler's War, and I want him for that. I want him." Turk's mustaches bristled, and the veins on his bull neck stood out in purple lines. "I want him more than anything I've ever wanted."

Having been silent, Wolf now put in a word. As second in command, he felt the need to exert a little authority.

"I don't like your mustache," he told Turk bluntly. "People will remember."

Turk, playing his game of the cool one, didn't flare up about the remark. Instead, he said, "There will be no witnesses, my friend."

Blake grinned, his lips slitted like a cat's before pouncing on prey. "No," he agreed, "we leave no eyes. It is our policy."

"Business?" queried Turk.

"Business."

There followed after that meeting a series of bloodthirsty robberies and raids in that pocket of the West, which left people shuddering. Family men carried shotguns to town when they took their families. Stage lines doubled their guards. Even the Army put extra men on, when payrolls were freighted from the East. There was no doubt who was responsible. Everybody knew the Kill 'em Alls were once more active. The trouble was, the gang became a gang in name only, because nobody lived to describe the killers. It was a horrible time. Anything of value was subject to the gang's violence, from stagecoaches to well-off ranchers. The country became an armed camp, and the Kills thrived.

Even McCall heard about them as far

south as Abilene. He cursed himself for not getting Blake, but it seemed more important to get cleared with the law. Now he wasn't so sure. Blake was the head of the Kills. With his death, the gang would fall apart—unless that hard one, Wolf, took over. It would probably be best to get both.

McCall thought about Lottie and worried. The Running B was a large spread, big enough to attract the gang. In addition, knowing Blake, it was possible the man knew she had harbored someone Blake very much wanted dead. The Kills leader might raid the ranch for vengeance alone.

The thought was disquieting, and McCall urged Dogs on at a faster pace than he should have.

"Sorry, hoss," he apologized, "but we have a double duty here. First, to get the law off my back, next to get back to Lottie, before . . ." He stopped here, not wishing to voice his fear aloud. The spoken words seemed to accentuate the danger, and he shivered involuntarily. Nothing, but nothing, must happen to Lottie Branch.

He reached Abilene in two weeks and put Dogs in a stable at once, with instructions for rubdowns and plenty of good grub.

Then he wired the mayor and sheriff of Postville. "I'm in trouble with the law for killing Scar," he penned. "Send wire telling who I am and why Scar is dead."

After supper, he lay down on his hotel bed for a rest. It was the first bed he'd had under him in some time, and it felt like feather heaven. He loosed a long sigh, like a horse contented after a feed of oats, and shut his eyes. He allowed the muscles in his strong frame to relax one by one, into a lazy complex of utter ease. He could sleep on the hard ground with no trouble, had done it off and on all his life, but there was nothing like a bed, when you got right down to it—even one with a mattress that smelled of spilled booze and cigarette smoke, and was stained with the bodies of grimy visitors past.

As he was about to drift off, the door slammed open rudely, a rattler striking without warning. A beady-eyed man with a sheriff's badge bounced into the room, followed by two husky deputies. They all had their weapons drawn.

"Up, feller," commanded the sheriff, "and keep your hands mighty visible."

The sheriff needn't have worried about McCall's getting up. He sprang into an upright position, like a cat jumping on a fence. He was up, before the sheriff's crisp words had time to zing off the walls.

"What's going on!" bellowed the man from Texas. "I haven't done anything here."

"No," agreed the sheriff surprisingly, "but we are gonna make sure you don't."

A third man entered. He was the telegrapher who'd sent McCall's message to Postville.

"That's him," he said. "That's the killer."

Without asking, McCall knew the story. The telegrapher had told the law about his telegram. It was probably his duty to have done so—McCall didn't know. He did know that he would like to have taken the man behind a barn and taught him a lesson in keeping-the-mouth-shut, because suddenly more complications cluttered his life. It was like trying to climb a mountain in a heavy rain—up two steps, down three.

"Come along," ordered the sheriff. "I'd hate for my boys to get rough."

"Aren't you going to let me explain?"

"Yes—behind bars."

McCall didn't resist, since resistance would have been useless. Where would he go if he escaped? The November weather was getting cold, for one thing, and he'd need a warmer outfit to travel the Plains. He had summer gear. If he made a successful break, he would still be at the mercy of great winds and freezing temperature.

Once inside the jail, the sheriff nodded. "Now you can tell your story."

"Scar was a killer," said McCall bitterly. "He and his partner, Blake, murdered my wife and child."

At the mention of Blake's name, the sheriff's eyebrows somersaulted. "Ain't he the head of that gang calls themselves the Kill 'em Alls?"

"The same."

The sheriff thought a minute. "I got me a letter here describes a man like you in that bunch." His voice turned truculent. "How's about it?"

McCall saw no sense in lying. His great hope lay in the answer he got from Postville. The truth could do no harm now.

"I joined the gang, because I was after Blake and Scar. But I wasn't certain it was them I wanted. I had to hear it from their own mouths. The only way I could do that was get with them."

"Sounds like a Ned Buntline story so far, mister. It's as full of holes as a target on an Army rifle range. My bet is you killed Scar, because of some disagreement."

"When we were on top of twenty thousand dollars?" McCall argued. "Wouldn't I wait till we got the money and got away? Seems like it would be then I'd settle a grudge."

The sheriff shrugged indifferently. "All I got to say is that telegram you're expecting better be good."

That, thought McCall, is exactly what I think. He felt like a coyote beleaguered by wolves. A total of three sheriffs had cornered him in the past weeks. None of them believed his story, and he couldn't blame them. It was highly improbable, but it was the truth. Only a good, strong voice from Postville could help him now.

He sat back on his bunk (were all jailhouse bunks so dirty?) and rubbed his jaw. There was nothing to do but wait . . . and wait. In the meantime Blake could be closing in on Lottie. Lon, the foreman, was a good man, and no doubt the Running B had good hands, but would they be willing to fight such as the Kill 'em Alls?

McCall groaned in frustration and clenched his fists until the knuckles popped. By nightfall there was no answer, nor was there any the following morning.

The sheriff noted the fact with a lawman's disdain for criminals.

"Who do you think you're fooling?" he demanded in irritation. "You better know, I got me a wire heading for Easton, and if I get word you killed a man there, back you go."

The sheriff scowled. "And I'll have to send a couple of men with you. And I got just two!" He spit on the floor. "Criminals! Oughta hang the lot just to see 'em dance."

The thought was not pleasant for McCall, since it put him in exact touch with the sheriff's feelings about outlaws. And he, McCall, was very much one at that moment. Should he be sent back to Easton, it would be probable—due to the sheriff's personal feelings about crooks and the fact that he was short on men—the trip would be short. McCall would, he had no doubt, try to "escape," and would be shot trying. Nor would there be a lawman in the entire country who didn't know what had happend, and understand.

That night was the slowest in McCall's history. He had once been forced to spend the night on a roof, when flood waters ravaged his ranch—that night had been ever-lasting, but not so long as this. He had once been cornered by several thugs during the Rustler's War—ten hours of holding them at bay. He thought that had been a "for-ever" time, but compared to this, it was a second in time.

He heard voices around midnight in the sheriff's office, then silence. The men, ex-cept for one guard, had gone home. The silence became oppressive, like the heavy atmosphere before a cyclone, and McCall found sleep an unlikely visitor. He wasn't afraid. That had nothing to do with it. He was worried about Lottie. In his mind, he was certain Blake would pay her a call. As for a hanging—or a shooting on the trail back to Easton—McCall had long since made up his mind. He would neither hang nor take lead without a fight.

Finally, McCall slept. He reconciled his mind to the fact that there was nothing he could do for himself, that his fate was in the hands of others, and he lay back on the grimy bunk and slept.

When he awoke, the sun was pouring through the window, casting stiff shadows on the floor. Voices rumbled in the office, and soon the sheriff himself faced McCall.

Behind him stood the telegraph operator and both deputies. The sheriff's face was cloudy, ready to rain.

He handed a sheet of paper to McCall. "Read it," the lawman grunted, "and if I ever saw a phony that's it."

McCall read: "McCall innocent of murder. Scar a member of the Rustler's War gang. McCall a deputy in that war. Turn him free . . ." It was signed by the mayor, the sheriff, and when McCall read the last signature, he understood why the telegram had taken so long. His good friends in Postville had gotten the governor himself to sign.

McCall grinned. "I guess," he said, "you have to let me go."

"Not on your life," the sheriff nearly shouted. "That could be a fake."

McCall bristled. He had been through a particular hell the night before, and he wasn't in the mood for the sheriff's suspicions.

"Then wire Postville yourself," he shouted. "Wire the governor. Get your own answers."

The sheriff, not a man to let anybody outshout him, hollered, "Oh, I will, fella.

Meantime," he issued a mean grin, "you cool your heels here."

Hours later, the sheriff of Postville confirmed the first telegram, and McCall was freed.

"Thanks for nothing," he told his jailers with more than a touch of anger. "Your pigheadedness might just have cost somebody her life."

"Get out of town," growled the sheriff, "before I throw you in the jug for insulting an officer of the law."

McCall spun away without another word. His fight was not with the sheriff, but somebody infinitely more dangerous— Blake. He went to a restaurant and downed a huge meal, and as he ate he noted the weather outside. The skies were dark with snow clouds, and frost had already bitten anything bare enough for its teeth to sink into. So he bought a pack horse and loaded the animal with warm clothing, blankets, and food. Then he saddled Dogs and, with the pack animal hitched to his saddle, set out.

His destination was the Running B, weeks off. The weather turned out to be more than just nasty. McCall had never experienced such viciousness from good old

Mother Nature. As soon as he left town, he felt the full force of the wind. It drove into him and his animals with hammering force, and never eased up. In the wind and the ominous, clouded skies, there was an enemy that could kill him. It would have been wise to have turned back to town and waited out the storm.

But McCall set his jaw, and thrust it into the invisible, deadly shafts. He meant to go on, no matter what it cost. Lottie Branch was far more important than his own well-being. He must—must—reach her as soon as he could!

Chapter Eleven

Lon was worried. The storm had been raging for a month, and the range was blown bare of dried winter grasses. The Running B herd was in danger of two calamitous events: starvation and freezing.

He was facing Lottie in the living room of the ranch house. A blaze warmed the fireplace and did its best to reach out into the room, but the blizzard outside kept pushing its warmth back. Lottie, dressed in heavy boots and clothing was thoughtful.

"So you think it's that bad, Lon?" she asked, more of a statement than a question.

"I can only guess, Lottie, but"—Lon

wrinkled his brow in painful acknowledgment of a fact—"I think it's a good one."

They'd been fighting the blizzards for a month. The entire Running B crew had been rounding up cattle for the market. The animals, it had become obvious, were doomed, and economics demanded that those who could stand the journey be delivered to the railhead.

But that endeavor was over. The storms persisted, and snow piled up in enormous drifts, stopped by so small a thing as a clump of grass. The clump grew into a giant. The whole northern Plains country was a mass of drifts and deep snow, and nobody, man or beast, could stand the drive to even more northern country where the railhead was.

As Lon spoke, he realized more and more that the Running B was doomed. He was sitting in a chair covered with a buffalo hide.

"Our critters need hides like these," said the Running B foreman, and he pointed to the buffalo fur.

Lottie nodded, and smiled ruefully. "Unfortunately, our stock comes from the south, Lon, with short hair."

Lon lapsed into a glum silence, broken finally, by the mistress of the Running B.

"Well," she said, "we've done all we can, my friend. We will just have to wait and see now. We have some money in the bank, thanks to the drive we did make. We can cover a few more payrolls, and then . . ." Lottie shrugged in frustration.

"Shall I say anything yet?"

"No. We'll keep the men long as we can."

Though the Running B had nearly 4,000 head of Longhorn Hereford cattle, a tough, meaty breed, Lottie could round up barely a thousand before the storms shut her down. The money these brought, coupled with what was in the bank, gave her enough for a payroll of three months.

"Unless the weather lets up," she advised Lon grimly, "I'm going to have to let the crew go. Better warn the boys in case they can find more permanent work."

It was a nice gesture on Lottie's part, but futile. There was no work on other ranches. All ranchers on the northern Plains were going through the same nightmare.

The storms refused to let up. It was as if angry gods, displeased with the hardscrabble life ranchers led, meant to punish them.

The ranchers met in Haystock to cuss and discuss the problem.

"We got 'er tough enough, 'thout this," was the general opinion.

The other predominant opinion was that every rancher would probably go broke if winter didn't give a little. The cattle, free and loose on the range as they were, had no protection, and were dying by the thousands.

Lottie rode out with Lon, whenever the weather broke enough to take the risk. What she saw was both horrifying and pit-iful. Cattle, frozen in their tracks, formed icy statues. They stood in deep arroyos to escape the wind, but the wind found them and turned them to stone in clusters. Many, at the verge of death, ribs sticking out like pine trees, as Lon put it, were shot to spare them further misery.

Lottie prayed for a letup, but the storms increased in fury. Huge balls of black clouds struck the land like great, clenched fists. Freezing temperatures, made more deadly by the driving wind, crept into every warm-blooded creature on the Plains. Not only did cattle perish, but antelope and elk, prairie dogs and rabbits as well. Nothing, except man, escaped, and even man perished. Lottie knew of several ranchers who ventured too far from the security of their homes and failed to return.

For some reason, she wished for McCall. She knew there was nothing he could do, but his large frame and logical mind would at least offer comfort. She wondered where he was and if he'd been successful in his quest for a pardon by the law. She wondered about that, and she prayed for it. She wanted McCall safe.

The man she prayed for was alive, but by no means safe. He was on the Plains, heading for the Running B, but progress was slow. He had been forced to seek shelter in towns along the way, sometimes pinned down by malignant storms for a week at a time. He fretted when delayed thus, and to pass the hours, curried both Dogs and the pack horse until they shined like burnished brass. He wondered if Lottie was safe, he worried that her stock might be dying, and, most of all, he worried about Blake. Had the man taken his vengeance yet? Or had the storms held him down. Perhaps there was some good in the storms, after all, if that were the case.

And it was the case. Blake and Turk Siderack were stopped by the storms. Their criminal activities slowed considerably. As Wolf put it, "I ain't freezin' my legs to no horse, not even for a million." The gang was lying low in Laramie. They'd all grown beards as disguises, and though not the perfect disguise, it worked as long as they didn't let the law get too good a look at them. For that reason, they never traveled together, and met secretly if plans were in order.

Both Blake and Siderack were aware of McCall's release. An operation as large as theirs required spies in every part of the country. The spies informed them of wealth being shipped and of suspicious people to watch out for—and others to rob and kill. The spies also kept information about McCall flowing, so that Blake and Turk knew just about, if not exactly, where their hated quarry was.

They also guessed where he was going.

"We'll just leave her be," said Blake. "She's bait. I got a couple men watching the ranch. When McCall gets there, we act."

Turk's straight-out mustache seemed to edge up at the tips, indicating a grin. "Just so we get him," he whispered, "just so we do, friend." He wanted the job over with, and then it was straight south into warm weather for him.

"Honey is a strong lure for any bee," Blake responded confidently. "He'll get there."

"We kill 'em all?"

"All."

"Quite a few hands there. The Running B is a big ranch."

"My boys let me know that quite a few of them are gone."

Turk was satisfied. "That will be easier."

"Yes. It will go well."

McCall, after a trip that left his face splotched from freezings time and again, arrived at the Running B. The trip had taken nearly two months, but he slogged through. He suspected that the ranch was under watch by Blake's spies, and considered avoiding the place altogether. He would send word to Lottie to meet him. But, somehow, Dogs and the pack horse kept going, and he arrived one morning, after clearing with Sheriff Tucker in Haystock. He didn't want the law badgering him or Lottie.

Tucker nodded when McCall presented

the telgram telling of his integrity, but was not impressed.

"Sure, it's signed by the governor," he pointed out. "But how do I know it ain't some kind of forgery?"

"Then get in touch with the law in Abilene," snapped McCall, his bones weary and face frozen was out of touch with his usual patience.

"You know that'll take a long, long time," the sheriff countered, with impatience of his own.

"So be it," growled McCall, "but until you prove I'm a liar, I'm free to go. I'm heading for the Running B, where I'm welcome." McCall was displeased with himself for sounding like a petulant schoolboy, but he'd had enough of the law for a while.

"You can be certain, I'll check you out," was the equally disgusted reply, then the sheriff's voice softened a bit. "They can probably use your help at the B."

"Meaning?"

"Meaning, that like everybody else in this blamed country, the B is busted. Lottie let all hands go, except Lon."

"It's that bad?"

"Worse."

"Worse?"

"Looks like the country might be wiped out, as far as cattle are concerned."

This was not exactly news to McCall. He'd seen the results of malignant weather on the way across the Plains, but he had no idea ranchers were sinking out of sight.

His heart raced when he pulled in sight of the Running B. Lottie was foremost in his mind, as she had been since he left Abilene. Now that the moment was close and he'd see her again, he found himself as nervous as a schoolboy. He who had faced deadly enemies in the Rustler's War without a thought, who had infiltrated the vicious Kill 'em Alls with its dozen killers, was faint-hearted now. A girl—no, a woman—haunted his heart and made him tremble.

He pulled Dogs to a stop in front of the ranch house. The wind had let up a bit, so spreads of snow were not, at the moment, snaking across the frozen ground. It was quiet. Too quiet. No cowhands shouted from the barn; no wrangler coaxed horses into being nice in the corral. The quiet was strange and unorthodox. Cowboys were among the most vocal professionals in the world, delighting in venting their opinions about everything from cattle to horses to women. But all was quiet. Not a sound, not a whisper greeted him. The few horses in the corral stared at him stonily, their interest noncommital. There were no cows in sight, nor had he seen any on the way from Haystock. There were strange lumps in the snow, and here and there a leg stuck up like a fencepost, stark and grim, but nothing was alive. No lowing cattle, no calves punching mother's bag for a meal. Nothing. The way had been silent and bleak.

McCall was a mixture of anticipation, nervousness, and somberness when he rapped on the door. There was a stir in the house, then the door swung open. Lottie stared at him, and her eyes filled with a great light.

"McCall!" she cried, and stepped forward involuntarily.

It was the most natural thing in the world, for him to take her to him, to press her to his chest, and to kiss her. It was as if this was something that had been arranged somewhere by the fates, and when the moment arrived, there was no hesitation.

"I hoped and prayed you'd come," she murmured, head leaning on his broad shoulder. "Oh, how I wanted that."

He kissed her again. "Looks like," he said gently, "I made it."

"And the law?"

"I'm clear."

"I knew you would be. I knew it, McCall."

"Tucker said you've been having hard times."

"Couldn't you tell?"

"Yes. The storms?"

"The storms have wiped out most of the ranchers in this part of the country. I'm nearly broke. Only Lon is left."

At that moment, Lon strode through the door. He stuck out his hand, and McCall took it.

"Outlaw or not," the foreman grinned, "I'm glad to see you, McCall. I think trouble is on the way."

"Well, he's not an outlaw," Lottie cried happily, then paused, her eyes serious. "Trouble? How can anything more happen?"

"I was out at the first line cabin just now, checking while the weather allows it." His voice was dry and rueful. "Even though there's nothing to check. Never saw a live critter, Lottie." He hesitated, then added, "And I seen a bunch of fellers coming, and one of them is that gent with the mustaches."

"Turk Siderack?"

"The same."

McCall's interest sharpened. "Was one a skinny fellow who maybe sat in lead?"

Lon thought, then nodded. "I think so. They was all done up in mackinaws and heavy clothes. Hard to tell, but I recognized that Turk feller all right."

"He's after you, McCall," interceded Lottie.

"That's what I mean," said Lon, "when I said trouble was on the way."

"We better go for Sheriff Tucker."

McCall shook his head. "No, I want Blake. He's mine. I've come a long way for him, Lottie."

A picture of his lovely wife and daughter lying in a pool of blood snapped to McCall's mind and fired him with a depth of hate no man could match.

"I want him," he said huskily.

"But what about Turk and the others? You can't stand them all off, and the sheriff wants Blake very much. There's a reward out for the whole gang, you know."

"No, I didn't know—and I don't mind that. It's him I want."

"And Siderack?"

"If he insists."

But Lottie was having none of that. In an aside, she told Lon to get the sheriff.

"But McCall might need help, Lottie. There's a dozen of 'em."

"Then go like the wind, Lon, but go!"

McCall had in the meantime, put both Dogs and the faithful pack horse in the barn. He spoke quietly to them, loving the two animals for enduring the great storms with him without balking once.

"Dogs," he joked, "don't be jealous if I give old Spot here"—a name he'd picked for the pack animal, because of a white mark on his rump—"a bit of attention. He is almost as good as you."

Dogs didn't pay the slightest attention. His nose was buried deep in the feed bag, as he munched the good quality of oats that the Running B stocked. McCall was so intent on his horses, he didn't hear Lon saddle up and leave.

After he tended his beasts, McCall checked his weapons. He now had a repeating rifle and his pistol. They were loaded, and he had plenty of ammunition. He carried them back to the house with him, ready for whatever, but he announced,

"Lottie Branch of the Running B, I am so hungry, I could eat snake bellies, topped off by buffalo chips. You got anything like that?"

The girl laughed. "Maybe I can do you a bit better. How about steak and eggs and fried potatoes and bread and coffee?"

"Good Lord, woman, have I died and gone to heaven?"

Lottie's eyes clouded. "Don't joke about dying. I don't think it's funny with them"— she nodded vaguely to the outdoors—"on the way."

McCall shrugged. In his heart was a fierce joy. He was about to meet the man he most wanted to see in the entire universe. The long trail was about to end, one way or another.

The man he thought about, Blake, the leader of the Kills, was thinking approximately the same thing. He was about to shoot down the man who had turned traitor, and who had killed his partner, Scar. In Blake's mind, the fact that he and Scar had murdered McCall's family didn't register as much as Scar's death. Scar was a valuable asset in the gang. McCall's family had been witnesses. The two women were killed for business purposes. Usually, the survivors lost all heart for further hostilities. It hadn't been so with McCall, and Blake could see he'd made a mistake. Still, business was business, and even business held its errors. This one had caused him some grief, but he meant to rectify that. Until McCall was dead, he'd be a thorn in his side.

There was in Blake also a fierce joy, the same as McCall was feeling. He anticipated the coming fight. He knew that the men at the Running B had been laid off, that there were only the woman, the foreman, and, now, McCall there. His contact in Haystock had filled him in. It would soon be over. He had waited a long time for this moment, and his vicious heart pumped as the adrenaline mounted in his scrawny body.

Wolf, the man who would be leader if Blake died, rode with his own thoughts. He wouldn't mind being head of the Kill 'em Alls. There was, to his mind, glamour in the title. He had sufficient anger and depraved morality to become a legend in the annals of western crime. Wolf knew this. There was in the man enough craving for the limelight to risk a public hanging. People would come for miles to see his death. They would bring picnic lunches, and children would roll hoops and it would be a gala gallows occasion. It would be an event people would remember for the rest of their lives, and they would tell their grandchildren about the day they saw Wolf, captain of the Kill 'em Alls go to his death with a grin and a wave of his hand.

As Wolf dreamed, Turk Siderack's thinking took a more practical turn. He wanted this business over. He had by now withstood thousands of miles of hard trail, months of storms that could freeze a man's soul, and months of a cold hatred for a man who had caused all of this discomfort. Turk wanted it over. He wanted to kill McCall and make sure the man knew who was killing him and why. He wanted to finish off witnesses, among them that girl, Lottie, she with the pretty face and wary eyes. He might have gone for her, but all thoughts of romance were dimmed by a long absence, and her connection with McCall. Too bad, but she had to die.

"I want the girl," he said, breaking into the silence.

"So do I," was Blake's response. He had a special reason for murdering women and children. Such a man held the respect of cutthroats he led. They could respect cold bloodthirstiness, the slaughter of the help-less. Blake knew this, and the slaughter of innocents had become part of his program to retain leadership. It was a matter of busi-ness.

"We'll see," grunted Turk Siderack.

"Yes."

And the one could see that the other was determined to have his way in this. It was a competition that Blake would not ordi-narily allow; they were too close to their goal now. It was not time to argue.

The buildings of the Running B came into view, and Blake raised his hand for a halt. Most of the men in gang had also served a hitch or two in the Army fighting Indians, and understood Army signals. They halted, waiting, a group of thin-faced thugs on horses, wanting loot and smelling blood.

"We'll burn the buildings," said Blake, "and kill everybody and every animal there. We will divide the take later. The loot will be divided. No individual will please himself, but *must* share."

The preciseness of this order, standard procedure in the gang, pleased Blake. It was spoken with Army crispness, and he knew his men. If the order was to share, that they would—most of it, anyway.

Blake turned his eyes to the distant buildings. The time had come. He raised his arm, and let it drop forward.

"Yo," said Blake. "Yo!"

And the gang moved forward to put in another day's work.

Chapter Twelve

McCall stepped out on the porch. His fierce anger drove him to meet Blake, and leave caution inside the house. He didn't want Lottie mixed up in what he considered his personal fight, but Lottie was having none of that, either. She stood at his side.

"You'll be killed," protested McCall. "Get back inside, I say."

"Do you think this bunch will leave me alive, McCall?" The girl was scornful. "Come on, man, those are the Kills. Do you know what they do to women and children and old people?"

McCall knew, and felt a chill run up his

back, like a cold snake. This was, he realized, not his battle alone. The girl was very much involved—it was a matter of life or death for her, too.

"I shouldn't have come here," he said savagely. "I might have guessed Blake would be keeping track of me."

"Don't worry about it," Lottie told him. "I want you here, McCall, no matter what happens."

He looked at the girl, and saw the love in her eyes. He saw the determination, the boldness, and the fight in them that had made her a successful rancher—before nature nearly wiped her out. He knew he had an ally in her, an ally for life, no matter what. He could have been an outlaw himself, and she would have backed him one hundred percent. She was a one-man woman, and he was that man. The knowledge drew another thrill along McCall's back, but this was a warm one, welcome to him, a caress of love.

"Well, at least go back, until I can talk to them," he said. "Where's Lon?"

"Gone for the sheriff."

For the briefest of moments, McCall showed impatience. "If that badge carrier gets here before I have my moment with Blake—I'll settle with you later."

"What you going to do, spank me?" was the retort, and McCall knew she was laughing at him. She had done what she felt was best. If he didn't like it, too bad. Lottie Branch, he was learning, was a mighty independent thinker.

The gang was now within a hundred feet of the house. McCall made them out clearly: Blake, Wolf, and the man Turk Siderack. He was curious about Siderack.

"Turk Siderack!" he called.

The man with the military mustache drew his horse to a stop. The others stopped with him. They sat stiff in their saddles, waiting for a signal from Blake to get it over with.

"I'm here," said Siderack evenly. He grinned, his yellow teeth a bizarre contrast against the dark hair on his upper lip. "At last."

"Your brothers had it coming," McCall informed him. "And, since you are a member of the Kills, I reckon you do, too."

Blake interrupted. "Not for you to say, McCall."

"Pitt to you, killer of women."

McCall saw, again, his wife and child

lying in the curious posture of death, still, still, never to move again unless by the hand of man. He saw their quiet forms on the ground, peaceful in death, but also blood-soaked—their blood. His rage and grief soared to a new height. Here was the man who had helped kill them. Here was the slime who had wiped out his family without so much feeling as he would give a snake.

He drew his pistol, and fired. He missed. In his fury, his aim was shaky, and he missed, but an immediate rain of lead flew back. He leaped at Lottie, and they tumbled through the open door of the house. McCall felt a tug at his leg, as he slammed the door shut. He knew he'd been hit, but counted himself lucky, since the injury didn't seem to be serious.

He raced to a window, broke out a pane, and fired back. The gang was dismounting and charging for the door, but McCall's shots, joined by those of Lottie with a Winchester repeating rifle, drove them to cover. There was a lull.

Then Blake called, "We'll let the girl go, if you turn yourself over to us peaceful. All's we want is you."

"Don't you dare," declared Lottie to the

man she had chosen for a life's mate. "You know they don't mean that."

McCall nodded. "Stick it up your nose, Blake," he shouted back. "How'd you ever get to be leader of such a gang? You're too stupid to lead a pack of mules."

A series of shots from the gang followed those remarks, but the house was built of cottonwood logs, long seasoned into a nut-hard toughness. The bullets thunked into it harmlessly. Unless the bullets went through the windows, they were useless.

"I have to get to them," decided McCall. "The law's coming, and I want Blake."

"You'll be killed if you go out there alone," protested Lottie, her eyes bright with alarm. "Don't, McCall, please don't."

"I have to. You know why I'm here. I would never forgive myself, if I didn't follow through now. I've got to chance it, Lottie."

The girl started to protest again, but saw in McCall's tense, stubborn rage that he would listen to nobody but himself. She realized that there was nothing she could do to stop him. He was right. He had come too far, lived too long with the horror in his memory to give up now. A settling must happen, and it must happen on a man-to-man basis. There was no other way. The law was after Blake and the Kills, but even if Blake were tried and hanged, McCall would never be satisfied. This was a blood-letting he would have to attend personally, or he could never be at peace.

She nodded, and asked, "What should I do?"

"Stay here, and shoot out the window. Shoot at anything, just to keep them occupied. I'm going out the back door."

"One quick kiss."

He met her lips briefly with his, touched her arm with his hand, met her eyes, and said, "I'll be back."

Crouching, he headed for the back door through the kitchen. Lottie fired with her Winchester, and kept firing, and the house was a huge drum that banged against the sky. McCall entered the kitchen and nearly bumped into one of the gang. He fired quickly, and the man dropped, but not before squeezing off a shot of his own. The bullet missed, but the damage had been done. McCall cursed. The gang knew his whereabouts now. He dashed into the open, expecting heavy fire, but reached the safety of a pile of firewood without anything happening. He wondered about that, and realized it would take the gang a few moments to chase around the house to the rear. His main fear was for Lottie, now. Blake and Turk would know she was alone, and could rush her. To prevent that, he stood up and fired in the general direction of the gang, shouting, "Come and get it. I got plenty!"

Blake heard the words, and nodded to himself in complete satisfaction. He wanted McCall first. The girl could be taken care of later.

"Go for him," he ordered his men. "But try to get him alive."

He led the way, followed closely by Turk.

Blake was surpremely happy. He had planned a long time for this. He was proud of himself for knowing McCall would show up at the Running B. A perfect setup. He was about to capture the man who had him thrown in jail. By so doing he, Blake, was exposed to the law. He had a midnight face until then, nobody knew what he looked like. Only his gang knew, and other witnesses were killed.

Now he was known, and Blake was angered over that. Further, the man they were about to get had put Scar under, and there was no better partner in the world than

Scar. He was much better than the mustachioed Siderack, who had, it seemed, declared himself a leader. Turk claimed he was leaving after this, but would he? The Kills were too good a money-making organization to pass up. Blake didn't trust the man. All criminals, as well he knew, were greedy, and greed could make a man ambitious. Well, there was a sure way to stop ambition. Blake had already decided to take no chances. After the Running B thing was over, he would kill Turk Siderack.

Turk, meanwhile, was thinking his own thoughts. He was determined to be the one to get McCall. He had come too far, endured too much, lost too much money, to allow anybody else to take him. McCall was, rightfully, his. He also had a blood relationship in this matter, which far outweighed any vengeance motives Blake might have. No, he would see to it that it was his bullet that ended McCall's life.

Turk Siderack smiled. He liked what was happening. He was happiest when death rode his shoulders.

McCall fired at the Kills as they rounded the corner of the house. His six-shooter clicked on an empty chamber, and he cursed himself for not bringing another weapon. He flipped open the cylinder of the .45 and flipped out the empty cartridges. Then he reloaded hastily, able to plug in only four, before Blake roared around the woodpile. His own pistol was aimed directly at McCall's heart.

"Got you," snarled Blake. He cocked his pistol. He wanted to take McCall alive; he wanted to torture the man who had caused so much trouble. He wanted to see him squirm and beg for mercy, before he finally killed him. But seeing McCall there, pistol half raised, Blake lost himself in the heat of the moment and fired. McCall felt the heavy slug tear into his shoulder, and he staggered back. McCall fired, but it was a blurry shot, and he missed.

There was another shot, but this one came from behind Blake. Blake staggered. A look of complete surprise smoothed his face, and he swung around drunkenly.

"You," he managed. "You!"

Then he pitched forward, and danced the death struggle on his side.

Turk Siderack loomed over the writhing body. His yellowed teeth never more in evidence.

Without a word, he leveled his weapon. McCall's vision had returned from the shock of Blake's slug and he saw Turk clearly. They fired at the same time, and once again, McCall was hit, but he had the satisfaction of seeing Turk stumble back. He saw the man try to lift his gun for another shot, so he fired again, and again Turk Siderack was hit. This time he flailed backward, his arms spinning like the blades on a runaway windmill. Then he collapsed, and joined his treacherous partner, Blake, in the short trail to eternal darkness.

At that moment, Wolf rounded the woodpile, firing as he came. McCall would have died at that moment, but for Lottie who fired from the house. Wolf spun around in his tracks, tried to right himself, then collapsed.

A startled silence followed the downfall of Wolf. The rest of the Kills darted behind protective barriers, as Lottie rushed to McCall's side.

"You hurt bad?" she cried.

"Can't tell," McCall answered honestly. In the heat of the fight, he didn't know. He could still move, and that was what counted. "Keep down," he told the girl. Then he nodded at the still body of Wolf. "And thanks for that."

The girl shuddered and turned her face

away. "I don't like what I did," she said, then added fiercely, "but nobody, not anybody, is going to take you away from me—not even if I have to—do that."

McCall nodded, but all the while he was waiting for another charge from the Kill 'em Alls. As he talked with Lottie, he listened for a move from them, some movement. He could hear them talking, deciding what to do. They had no leader now, and decisions had to be made by group.

Suddenly, one cried, "It's the sheriff!"

And another one yelped, "And he's got a dozen men."

Sheriff Tucker rode in at a swift gallop firing as he came. Lon was with him, also firing, and a short, dense fight followed, in which two more Kills were added to the lists of eternity, and one man in the posse was wounded.

McCall and Lottie remained ready, but stayed clear of the fight. They watched as Tucker, along with his deputies and Lon, rounded up the rest, and all at once it was over.

"Well," said McCall, "well," and then he passed out from shock and loss of blood.

McCall didn't die from his wounds, and

when he was feeling better, he teased Lottie about that.

"Suppose Old Man Death came for me," he asked, "how would you have stopped him?"

"I don't know," was the grim reply, "but you can bet your saddle I would have."

And McCall had no doubt the girl would have found a way. He found himself watching her when she wasn't looking. What a great thing fate had done putting them together. She was the only woman in the world who could have come into his life. The memory of Belle, his blue-eyed wife, and his lovely daughter, Katherine, would never fade, but the pain of their unnecessary deaths would gradually heal with Lottie in his life.

Though his wounds hadn't taken his life, he would limp for the rest of his days, but a limp was worth the price. The two terrible men who had shaken his very existence were dead. They, and Turk Siderack, would never again murder anybody. Oh yes, the limp was a small price to pay.

He proposed marriage to Lottie so suddenly, it even startled him, and his proposal was unorthodox.

"I think we can restock," he said one

spring morning, when the breezes blew fair, and the skies were warm.

"We haven't the money," the girl replied, reflecting.

"I have some, and surely we can borrow on this property. The Running B is a large spread."

And then Lottie Branch looked at him, and her eyes were happy and laughing.

"Why, I do declare," she said gently, "I believe I'm being proposed to."

McCall stared at her perplexed, and then caught it.

"I said 'we', didn't I?"

"Yes, McCall, you did that, and I said 'we', too. Guess that means 'us', right?"

"Right," said McCall, and he kissed her. "Right."

Lon, was the best man at the wedding, and Sheriff Tucker gave the bride away.